"The first treat is for old time's sake. You're on your own from there," she quipped, thinking how nice it was not to have to work at conversation for a change.

It had always been like that with Dade. Easy. Light. Fun. *When they were young*, she corrected. High school had been another matter altogether.

Things changed. And so did people.

The serious blue eyes Dade had possessed as a child were even more intense now. As easy as conversation had been between them all those years ago, neither had spoken about their demons—demons that grew and changed people over time. Demons that could make a man sign up to travel halfway around the world to fight a monster he couldn't see.

"It's good seeing you again, Dade," she said, finally looking up and realizing what a mistake that was. Because he was looking, too. And the way he was looking made her body ache like it hadn't in far too long.

"You, too, Carrie."

Neither made a move to leave right away.

TEXAS GRIT

USA TODAY Bestselling Author
BARB HAN

HARLEQUIN INTRIGUE®

To my editor, Allison Lyons, for being a dream to work with—thank you! To my agent, Jill Marsal, for always having the right words of encouragement—thank you!

To my children, Brandon, Jacob and Tori, who inspire me to be the best version of myself every day. I'm eternally grateful. Whether we're up late carving pumpkins or cheering each other on in our daily adventures (some might say antics) I'm always grateful for our close relationships. Brandon, welcome to the 1m challenge. I'd wish you luck but since you're one of my competitors…game on, buddy! I love you all so very much!

And to John, for laughing no matter how silly we get and for jumping in with both feet for every challenge no matter how crazy. I can't imagine a better partner in crime and in life. I love you!

ISBN-13: 978-1-335-52644-1

Texas Grit

Copyright © 2018 by Barb Han

Recycling programs for this product may not exist in your area.

Printed in U.S.A.

USA TODAY bestselling author **Barb Han** lives in north Texas with her very own hero-worthy husband, three beautiful children, a spunky golden retriever/ standard poodle mix and too many books in her to-read pile. In her downtime, she plays video games and spends much of her time on or around a basketball court. She loves interacting with readers and is grateful for their support. You can reach her at barbhan.com.

Books by Barb Han

Harlequin Intrigue

Crisis: Cattle Barge

Sudden Setup
Endangered Heiress
Texas Grit

Cattlemen Crime Club

Stockyard Snatching
Delivering Justice
One Tough Texan
Texas-Sized Trouble
Texas Witness
Texas Showdown

Mason Ridge

Texas Prey
Texas Takedown
Texas Hunt
Texan's Baby

The Campbells of Creek Bend

Witness Protection
Gut Instinct
Hard Target

Rancher Rescue

Harlequin Intrigue Noir

Atomic Beauty

Visit the Author Profile page at Harlequin.com.

CAST OF CHARACTERS

Carrie Palmer—This sweet shop owner with a difficult past has made good with her life—a life that someone is insistent on taking away from her.

Dade Butler—This Butler twin is back from the military and trying to figure out his place in the family now that his larger-than-life father is gone.

Nash Gilpin—This festival worker seems obsessed with spending time with Carrie. How far will he go to force her into his life?

Samuel Jenkins—This keeps-to-himself neighbor of Carrie's seems to know an awful lot about her whereabouts. How far is he willing to go to get to know her better?

Brett Strawn—This ex-boyfriend isn't taking Carrie's rejection lightly. Just how far will he go to get her back?

Sheriff Clarence Sawmill—This sheriff might be in over his head with a high-profile murder to solve and a town in chaos.

Maverick Mike Butler—Even in death this self-made Texas rancher has a few cards left to play.

Chapter One

Carrie Palmer planted her shoulder against the back door of her cold-treats shop and, with a grunt, gave it a good shove. The latch could be tricky and required a certain touch. Humidity always caused the solid wood door to swell. It was August in south-central Texas, with the threat of rain hanging in the air. She twisted the key and listened for the snick of the lock.

The heat combined with a successful annual week-long festival had brought another day of fantastic sales to Carrie's Cold Treats. Aside from an annoying festival worker who seemed bent on dating her, this year's AquaPlay Festival and Cattle Run had gone off without a hitch. People were laughing again, and everyone in Cattle Barge needed the distraction. The town could use a sense of normalcy after being turned upside down for the past couple of weeks following the murder of a prominent family's patriarch, Mike Butler, a.k.a. Maverick Mike.

The man who was notorious for living large and

on his own terms had made national news after being found gunned down on his beloved ranch.

Every time she thought about his son, Dade, her heart squeezed. She'd heard that he'd been discharged from the military recently and had only been in town a few weeks. She could only imagine what her childhood friend was going through. Not only had his father been killed in a bizarre manner that had caused a media frenzy *and* an attempt had been made on his sister's life, but an adult child no one had known about had been summoned to town, bringing with her a murderous ex-boyfriend. Carrie shuddered, because after her recent breakup with Brett Strawn had blown up, he'd made terrible threats— threats she knew in her heart he couldn't mean. Before she would've chalked them up to him being emotional, a temporary reaction to the disappointment of a relationship ending. Now, she worried.

With Brett, it probably was just the heat of the moment that had him saying words she knew he'd regret when he had some time to think about them. And yet her problem was nothing in comparison to Dade's. Her heart went out to him as she watched his worst nightmares play out in the news, wishing she had some way to contact him. Even at nine years old, he'd had the most serious blue eyes beneath thick, curly, sandy-blond hair.

Theirs had been an unlikely friendship. His family was one of the most prominent in Texas, while she had no parents, moving from group home to a distant relative's house and then back into foster care through the early part of her life. Funny how little kids never noticed how much or how little money another kid's family had. Interesting how much that changed later in life. By the time she'd returned to the same high school after being relocated and bounced in and out of another home, everything had changed. Dade had grown into his athletic frame. He'd become popular and, outside of a few glances in her direction, she was sure he didn't even remember her name.

It was dark outside. She normally closed at dusk, but the AquaPlay Festival broke down at sunset and she'd agreed to stay open late to accommodate all the children not quite ready to wind down on a summer night. At least her business was working for her, even though it seemed like everything else in her life was standing on shaky ground. She'd hoped to find a home in returning to Cattle Barge to open her store. But she felt just as much an outsider here as she had everywhere else she'd lived since college.

The overwhelming feeling that someone was watching caught Carrie off guard. This feeling was a little too familiar since her relationship with Brett had ended a couple of weeks ago, and she often thought she could feel him watching her.

She tried to shake it off, figuring her heightened emotions had to do with the breakup, the words that had been spoken out of anger. And the dozens of apology texts that she had yet to read all the way through, let alone answer.

"Beautiful night," a male voice boomed from behind, startling her. He was close, and she hadn't heard him walk up.

"What are you doing back here, Nash?" A chill raced through her and her fingers tightened around her key ring as she pulled the key out of the lock. She whirled around and had to back up against the wooden door to put some space between her and the tall, thick-around-the-middle festival worker. He brought his hand up against the door, trapping her on one side. His long hair was soaked with sweat after breaking down and loading up the rides. He wore a stained tank top underneath a button-up denim shirt that had half the sleeves cut off. Threads frayed over thick forearms used to lifting heavy equipment.

"Festival's over. Thought you might like to spend some time together before I leave town." The smell of alcohol on his breath assaulted her as he leaned closer. She held her breath. He'd stopped by three times over the course of the weekend to ask her out. Each time she'd declined. She'd been crystal clear. There was no doubt in her mind that he hadn't some-how misinterpreted her rejections, and standing there any longer would cause her to pass out. "Or, maybe I'll find someone worth sticking around for and get a local job."

"It's late. I have to get home and let my dog out."

Carrie ducked under his arm and tried to sidestep him, blowing out a breath in the process. He moved with her, blocking her, and the hairs on the back of her neck stood on end.

Nash was big. Too big. Fighting him off would be a challenge. She palmed the small can of pepper spray attached to her key ring and flicked the leather cover open using her thumb, hoping she wouldn't need to use it. As long as she was wishing, she might as well go for it and wish she was already in her car.

The back parking lot was lit by a single light in the far corner. Out of habit, she'd parked in her usual spot behind the building. Regret stabbed her that she hadn't realized how dark it would be after extending her hours. Or how vulnerable she'd be walking to her car alone after she sent her employees home early, reassuring them she could close up by herself with no problem. The festival had ended two hours ago and everything was quiet—everything but the sounds of her pounding heart rushing in her ears.

"What about a movie first?" The cinema was at the end of the strip shopping center, and as much as Carrie liked the idea of being around people right now—lots of people—she didn't want to give false encouragement to a man who gave her the creeps.

She strained to hear voices, anything that might signal life was near, but was met with silence save for the sounds of Nash's heavy alcohol-infused breaths. If she got lucky, a movie would end and people would exit the cinema. She really hoped so, because she might need the help. As it was she doubted anyone would hear if she screamed, and Nash seemed to realize it, too, as a show of yellow teeth stared back at her.

"I've been working extra hours and haven't been home since lunch. Like I said, my dog needs to go out or I'm afraid she'll have an accident." Carrie looked up and didn't like what she saw in Nash's eyes. She flicked the safety off the pepper spray. Experience had taught her that she'd get some in her eyes, too, and hers started watering just thinking about the burn. Her lungs would seize and her chest would ache. But it would give her the edge she needed to get to her car, where she could lock herself inside.

Even at night, the August temperatures in Cattle Barge were in the high nineties. Sweat beaded on Carrie's forehead, a mix of fear, adrenaline rush and sweltering heat. Experience had also taught her not to show her emotions when facing down a bully, no matter how shaky she was on the inside.

Carrie looked straight into the man's eyes, and her heart skipped a beat at what she saw behind them. She resigned herself to a fight and fisted her free hand.

He slicked his tongue across his bottom lip and made a move to grab her.

She screamed as she brought the pepper spray toward his face.

"Everything okay here, Carrie?" The sound of

Samuel's voice was a welcome reprieve, like a soaking rain in the desert on a hot day.

Nash took a step back and turned his attention to her neighbor, sizing him up. "We're just talking."

Carrie used the distraction to dart toward her savior. He was a quiet guy in his late twenties, or maybe early thirties, who'd moved in with his elderly aunt in the same cul-de-sac as Carrie last fall. She presumed he'd moved to Cattle Barge to help his aging aunt, but she wasn't sure because she'd been busy with the shop and only interacted with a few people in town on a personal level. Personal level? Carrie would laugh if anything about that or this situation was actually funny.

"I'm so glad you're here." She grabbed his arm, noticed he was shaking, and an icy chill raced down her spine. She withdrew her hand, chalking up the reaction to overwrought emotions. Nash seemed to realize immediately what she already knew. Samuel was no match. He was close to her height and had no muscle mass, but he'd distracted the worker and that was good enough for her to make an escape. Between the two of them, she had a chance of getting out of this unscathed. She wouldn't look a gift horse in the mouth.

"Walk me to my car," she said to Samuel, dodging Nash's attempt to catch her arm.

Her neighbor shot the worker a look that was probably meant to scare him.

"Keep walking," Carrie told Samuel in a low voice.

"The lady and me were trying to have a conversation," Nash said. Based on the nearness of his voice, he wasn't more than a step or two behind them.

Could they make it to her car without an altercation?

"It's okay. Just keep our heads down and feet moving." She didn't want to provoke Nash any more.

Ten more feet and she'd be home free.

A callused hand gripped her shoulder, pinching hard, and she suppressed a yelp.

Samuel spun to his left to face off with Nash.

"She's with me," Samuel squeaked out, his voice shrill. He was trying to be a hero and was clearly not cut out for the job, because she could feel him trembling next to her. His skin had gone sheet white, and beads of sweat trickled down his forehead.

Like a shark zeroing in on a vibration of fear, Nash took a threatening step toward Samuel.

"Back off, little man," Nash demanded, his rough hand clamping around Carrie's arm.

She jerked it free and brought up the pepper spray. Nash caught her arm in time to stop her from aiming at his eyes.

"Carrie, is that you?" A dark rumble of a voice boomed from the end of the alley, and all three of them froze. She recognized who it belonged to immediately. Dade Butler's voice made her heart thump a little faster, and for very different reasons than being scared. The inappropriateness of her reaction to him caught her off guard, especially after all this time.

"Dade," she said, her voice sounding as desperate as she felt.

"Everything okay here?" Dade had to be at least six foot four, with a body built for athletics. Ripples of solid muscles were apparent underneath his white T-shirt and low-slung jeans. He seemed to size up the scene accurately, based on the deep wrinkle on his forehead and the fact that he was frowning.

"Yeah, why wouldn't it be?" Nash threw his hands up in surrender. "I was just leaving."

Samuel stepped between Carrie and Dade as though sizing up a new threat.

"It's definitely better now that you're here," she said to Dade to calm some of Samuel's tension. The message? Dade was a friend. Samuel just got the muscle he needed to avoid getting his face bashed in. He should be grateful instead of tense.

Nash seemed to take the hint, backing away before heading toward the cinema with a few choice words mumbled just loud enough to hear.

"How long has it been since the last time I saw you?" Dade asked Carrie, his eyes intent on Nash.

She stepped away from Samuel and toward the sound of Dade's voice as a sensual shiver rocketed through her.

"Too long." She hadn't seen him since the news

of his father broke and hadn't talked to him in years. She could never forget that voice, and even though dark circles cradled his still-too-serious crystal-blue eyes, he looked damn good. She turned to Samuel, whose body language was even tenser now. "Thank you so much for stepping in when you did. I don't know what I would've done if you hadn't shown up. I'm good from here, though, so you don't have to stick around."

The quiet neighbor didn't respond as he eyed Dade up and down. A glint of metal in his hand reflected in the light as he turned to face her. For the first time, she noticed that Samuel was hiding a knife. She appreciated that he was trying to help her and, sadly, they might've needed the weapon to fight off Nash. Between Samuel's knife and her pepper spray, they might've had a prayer. But the festival worker seemed to know better than to try to take on Dade.

"Everything all right?" Dade's brow arched as he seemed to process Samuel's resistance to leave.

Samuel still seemed to be looking at everyone as a potential threat.

"It's okay. I'm fine now. Dade's a friend of mine," Carrie said to Samuel. These were probably the most words she and Samuel had exchanged, and she was grateful he'd appeared when he did. It was probably adrenaline that had him still tense and ready to defend. He was somewhat awkward, and she figured he'd most likely dealt with his fair share of bullies in his lifetime, being on the scrawny side. The thought made her feel sorry for him. She knew what it was like to be pushed around and unable to defend herself. An angry riptide pulled at her thinking about it, about a past that had left her helpless. She dismissed thoughts that brought her back to that place where she was an innocent girl, fighting off someone who was supposed to be protecting her.

She shook off the reverie, focusing on Samuel. He nodded and seemed like he wanted to say something, but whatever it was died on his tongue. He settled on, "Good night, Carrie."

He seemed so sad, and she wanted to do something to thank him. From the way he carried himself, she doubted he'd stood up for himself or anyone else for most of his life and it had taken a lot of courage for him to do what he'd done. "Stop by the shop tomorrow for an ice cream on the house, okay?"

"Thanks." He smiled and she noticed his lip twitching—a nervous tic? Poor guy. He really was distressed, and she was even more grateful he'd tried to help. She'd send him home with a gallon of her signature ice cream blend for his aunt, too.

"'Bye, Samuel." She stepped into a friendly hug with Dade, ignoring the shivers racing through her body with contact.

"What was up with him?" Dade pulled Carrie against his chest, and she felt how truly muscled he was. His sandy-blond hair and serious blue eyes made for one seriously hot package. And those were all things former friends weren't supposed to think about each other. Notice, maybe, but not have a visceral reaction to.

"I really appreciate what you did after all these…" She diverted her gaze. In his arms, it was a little too easy to forget the awkwardness she'd felt toward him since high school. She pulled back, because thinking clearly while being barraged with his clean and spicy male scent made her pulse erratic.

Carrie was tall—not Dade tall, but tall—with midnight-black hair and tight curls that had minds of their own on humid days. She'd tamed them today with a straightening iron and had no idea why she was thinking about what her hair looked like after what had just happened. Stress caused her thoughts to bounce around, she reasoned.

"Are you shaking?" Dade asked.

"I guess so. That whole situation was stressful, but I'm fine now," she said a little too quickly. She wasn't okay. Recent events with Brett had her off-balance, and Nash had really done a number on her insides. "Nash has been hanging around the shop and tonight he had alcohol on his breath."

Dade's hand found hers, like they were still kids and running across the playground—which was as much as the action probably meant to him. It caused her heart to beat wildly against her chest.

She chalked her out-of-control reaction up to the stressful encounter with Nash; his eyes had told her everything she needed to know about his intentions.

"What was going down a few minutes ago?" With Dade next to her, she should be able to relax, and she could in some ways, because he'd just saved her from what could've turned out to be a very bad situation. One that brought a few harsh memories threatening to crash down around her and reduce her to tears.

She couldn't help but shudder when she thought about how close she'd been to history repeating itself. Well, now she was twenty-seven, not fourteen.

Dodging those heavy thoughts, she looked at Dade instead.

"That festival worker cornered me, and it got awkward. He's been asking me out all week, but I refused, so I guess he decided to take matters into his own hands before he left town." Hearing the words brought on another wave of anger.

A grunt tore from Dade's throat, but he didn't immediately speak, even though his jaw muscle ticked. "Tell me everything that happened."

"He surprised me in the parking lot when I was closing up the shop. Things got a little weird and, luckily, one of my neighbors happened to be near. Samuel must've heard my voice or something, because he showed up just in time to distract Nash. I'm so glad the festival's over so I won't have to deal with that guy again. He'll be long gone by morning."

A dark look crossed Dade's features and for a split second she thought she'd imagined it. "If I'd known, I would've been less friendly."

That was him being friendly? She'd hate to see someone on his bad side. "I'm just relieved it's over."

His eyes darkened anyway, and that jaw muscle bulged again. "Only because I showed up. What if I hadn't?"

She almost pointed out that Samuel had, too, but she knew he couldn't have held Nash off for long.

"It's my fault. I should've parked out front. Out of habit, I parked in back. I don't usually close up the store after dark." Thinking just how close the call had been caused her to shudder again.

"Don't blame yourself for being harassed by a jerk." Dade's free hand fisted. Tension radiated from him in waves. "Did he physically threaten you?"

"He had me trapped against the wall before Samuel arrived." The whole experience had tipped her off-balance, and she wasn't thinking straight. She should be angry, not scared. Too many memories haunted her, bringing her back to that defenseless fourteen-year-old girl she'd been when her foster father had abused her. Well, she was a woman now and could stand up for herself, and she sure as hell didn't need to make excuses for Nash or blame herself.

"I think it's best if I take you to the sheriff's office to give a statement," he said with calmness to his tone and something else… Possessiveness?

She really was imagining things now.

Shock was wearing off, and the adrenaline rush was making her hands shake. "I appreciate the offer."

"I don't trust Nash." Dade's jaw clenched as he scanned the area.

He was right. She glanced around. Nash could be anywhere, hiding, biding his time in order to make another move.

DADE RAKED HIS hand through his hair. He'd seen the look in the festival worker's eyes, and he hadn't liked it. Thankfully, Carrie's neighbor had been there to serve as a distraction until Dade could get things under control. The neighbor registered as a little odd, but Dade was grateful Samuel had been there to slow Nash down. Dade and Carrie went way back, and the thought of anything happening to her sat like a hot poker in his gut.

Seeing her shell-shocked and pale was like a physical punch, and his past shame roared to the surface. He hadn't helped her in high school like he should've, but there was nothing stopping him now. Besides, she wasn't thinking straight or she would've already come up with the idea of filing a complaint. Another reason leaving her alone wasn't a good idea.

"My truck is parked this way." He motioned toward the end of the alley.

She glanced at her sedan and then at him. "I don't

know, Dade. I'm tired. Part of me thinks I should just go home and try to forget this night ever happened."

"This guy could harass a woman in the next town he's in. We don't know anything about his background or if the festival vetted him out before he was hired. He could have a record and he might escalate if we don't nip this in the bud."

Carrie stayed quiet, standing in the back alley. The thought of a man forcing himself on her hit Dade in a very dark place.

Finally, she nodded and took in a sharp breath. "You're right. Let's go."

Dade ignored the fact that holding her hand felt different now. Of course it would—they weren't nine-year-olds playing tag at school. Her hand was softer and more delicate, especially in comparison to his. He spent most of his time outdoors, first in the military and now on the family ranch, where he'd always been hands-on. His showed the long hours he spent in the elements. She didn't seem to mind.

Electricity pulsed through him at the point of contact, but it couldn't be more misplaced. She needed a friend, and the last thing he needed was another complication in his life. Besides, how many times had he vowed to explain himself to Carrie if he got the chance? Years had gone by and he hadn't seen her. He'd been back for a few weeks now, and he'd come up with a million excuses for not telling her what he'd really want to say to her all those years ago when he'd been a jerk instead.

There were some wounds that ran so deep not even time could heal.

Chapter Two

All the words Dade had wanted to say to Carrie since high school died on his tongue. Too many years had passed and, his own guilt aside, she might not want to think about what had happened anymore. Besides, she'd escaped an assault tonight and he could clearly see how rattled she was. This wasn't a good time to bring up more pain.

"I completely forgot to ask what you were doing in the alley," Carrie said, stretching her legs in his truck as she fastened her seat belt.

"Trying to stay away from the media while I picked up the bronze statue my family donates to the festival." He turned the key in the ignition, and the engine hummed to life.

"Oh, right. The cattle run kicks the festival off." Her shoulders were still tense, her posture defensive.

"And is part of the closing ceremony, which is why I'm here carrying on the family tradition," he added. Being a Butler came with a price.

"I heard you left town for a few days after news of your father broke." Carrie gave him the most sincere look of compassion. "I'm sorry for your loss, Dade."

Those words spoken with such sincerity threatened to crack the casing in his chest. Dade couldn't afford to go there, so he focused on Carrie instead. Her lime-green shorts and cream-colored halter highlighted soft-looking pale skin. Taupe ankle boots—at least that's what they'd called that same color of paint when he'd had his house redone—showed off her calf muscles, and Dade reminded himself that he shouldn't be noticing any of those things about his friend.

"The Mav and I weren't the closest, but his being gone leaves a huge hole at the ranch." Dade thanked her for her sympathy. He gripped the steering wheel and navigated his truck away from the back street and onto Main. For the first time it struck him at how odd it must seem that he called his father Mav instead of Dad or Father like everyone else. But then, nothing about being a Butler made his life normal.

"When did you get back?" She pushed a few curling tendrils of hair from her face as she crossed those long legs.

"A few days ago," he said, adding, "Seemed like I was needed here with the attempt on my older sister's life and then finding out about having a sister we never knew existed."

"I read about what's been happening with your

family. Finding out you have another sister must've been a shock. And then her life was in jeopardy. Right?" she asked.

"Madelyn had an ex-boyfriend with a violent streak who tracked her down and attempted to kill her," he said. "We're damn grateful the criminals in both cases have been caught."

"Neither was connected to your father's murder?" Carrie asked.

"We thought Ella's might have been at first. Now, we know different. The Mav's killer is still at large. Every new threat against the family has more reporters descending on Cattle Barge."

"How's everyone doing?" Carrie asked.

"It's been rough."

"I can imagine." The note of compassion in her voice struck him, threatening to shed light in a dark place hidden behind layers of anger, frustration and regret.

"But we're finding a new normal. Everyone's looking out for each other." Dade needed to armor up, and the best way to do that was to redirect the conversation. "The sheriff will need a description and the name of the guy from the alley."

"That's not a problem. Unless… Actually, I don't know his last name. He introduced himself as Nash, and I never asked for his last name." Her voice was still shaky. "He gave me the creeps every time he came into the shop."

"A first name and description will go a long way toward helping the sheriff find him. If memory serves, the workers usually leave town early in the morning. Sheriff Sawmill or one of his deputies should have no problem locating this guy tonight." How many men by the name of Nash could be employed by the festival?

Carrie's cell buzzed inside her purse, and the unexpected noise caused her to jump.

"Sorry." She stuck her hand inside the bag and came up with her phone. After checking the screen, she refused to take the call.

"Does Nash have your number?" Dade doubted it, but the question had to be asked.

"I wouldn't give personal information to a stranger." Her indignant tone said he'd offended her.

"He might've gotten it from someone else or the internet," he offered by way of explanation.

"The phone call was my ex-boyfriend," she stated with the kind of emphasis on the *ex* that said there was a story there.

Dade hadn't thought to ask if there was someone special in her life. It made sense there would be, with her looks. A burst of light zapped his chest at the thought that she was single.

"We broke up recently, and he didn't take it well." Her cheeks flushed, and he wondered if he was making her feel uncomfortable talking about her relationships. He tried not to think about his, although the wounds were still fresh.

"How bad was it?" he asked.

"He said things I know he didn't mean. He just needs time to cool off." She shrugged it off, like it didn't bother her, but he could tell by her tone that it did.

"That's nothing to take lightly." Considering one of his siblings had just been targeted by a murderous ex-boyfriend, Dade figured he owed Carrie a warning. "What happened?"

"Brett said a few things he didn't mean. He was hurt and it came out as anger," she defended. "He's most likely trying to apologize. Things got a little heated."

"It's none of my business, but I wasn't kidding. Take his threats seriously." He pulled into the parking lot of the sheriff's office and found a good spot. There was a flurry of activity. A news reporter spotted them and made a beeline toward his truck. Damn. He hadn't anticipated this, but he should've. Seeing Carrie again threw him off-balance. "We could drive around the block a few times until the swarm calms down."

"It'll be fine." Her voice sounded anything but.

Flashes started going off through the truck windows, blinding Dade.

Carrie's arm came up to shield her eyes.

"I'd understand if you didn't want to be seen with me right now," he offered.

She touched his hand, and the contact sent electricity rocketing through him, searching for an outlet. "This is awful."

"Yep," he agreed. "They're camped out everywhere. I take a breath and it's on the news with some shrink or expert analyzing it."

"I've seen some of the coverage. No one should have to go through this." Carrie took in the kind of breath meant to fortify someone. Dade should know. It was a little too familiar. He'd done the same countless times since this whole ordeal began.

From the outside, their family probably did look perfect. No one knew the real truth. And it was too late to change the past.

"I'm ready whenever you are," she stated with a squeeze.

"Keep your face down and feet moving. I'll meet you around the back of the truck." He shoved his door open, pushing back the swarm, and then hopped out. Making his way to the back of the truck proved a challenge with all the cameras in his face, but he took his own advice. The brim of his Stetson blocked out some of the shocking blasts of lights that had the effect of fireworks being lit inches from his face.

A sense of calm settled over him when he looked up and saw Carrie moving toward him. Something felt very right in that moment. He chalked it up to nostalgia. Losing his father had him wishing he could go back. Change the past. He couldn't. So, it wouldn't do any good to make useless wishes.

Dade ignored the stirring in his chest that tried to convince him being around her again was a good idea.

"Take my arm." He held it out, and she took it. More of those frustrating zings of electricity coursed through him. *Way to keep the hormones in check around a beautiful woman, Butler.*

Reporters tried to follow him and Carrie inside the lobby, but a deputy quickly reacted, forcing them outside.

In the next minute, he and Carrie were being ushered into a hallway. He recognized the building all too well. He'd been there countless times since his father's murder. Always with the same result—no solid leads. A conference room had been converted into a makeshift command center where volunteers took shifts answering phones, jotting down leads. At least a dozen intake spots were set up around the long mahogany conference table. The room sounded like a Jerry Lewis telethon with the constantly ringing phones, hushed voices and volunteers with their heads hunkered down, speaking quietly into receivers.

The sheriff's office was large, simple. There was a huge desk, also mahogany, with an executive chair and two flags on poles standing sentinel on either side. A picture of the governor was centered in between the poles. Two smaller-scale leather chairs nestled near the desk. A sofa and table with a bronze statue of a bull with rider sitting astride it—commissioned by Dade's father—sat to one side of the room. Dade had been surprised to see the statue in the sheriff's office. But then, Mike Butler always had a few cards up his sleeve, and he'd been a complicated man.

Dade's oldest sibling, his sister Ella, kept talking about how she felt like their father was still watching over the family. She'd gotten closure from a note their father had given her days before his death. Dade was happy for his sister—finality and peace were two very good things—but his relationship with the old man couldn't have been more different. And he'd known the minute his father snatched a toy away from him at age seven and told him to quit wasting time and get to work that his father didn't look at him in the same light.

Expectations for Mike Butler's sons took on a whole new level. Dade and his twin brother, Dalton, had endured, not enjoyed, childhood. Both had been forced to grow up fast. And neither could really wrap his mind around the fact that the big presence that was their father was gone. A pang of regret hit Dade. He wished he could go back and have the conversation he'd needed to have with his father. Now it was too late.

"I wish I had news for you," the sheriff started as he took his seat in his executive swivel.

More useless wishes, Dade thought.

"I'm not here to talk about my family's case." Dade tried to mentally shake himself out of his reverie. Chewing on the past wouldn't make it taste better. Reality was bitter. His father was gone and their relationship was beyond repair. Case closed.

Dade focused on the sheriff, noticing the wear and tear on his features as his office continued to be inundated with phone calls, questions and leads about the Mav's murder. Deep lines bracketed the sheriff's mouth, and worry grooves carved his forehead.

"Would either of you like a cup of coffee before we get started?" Sheriff Sawmill asked, gripping his own mug of still-steaming brew. There was a packet of Zantac on top of his desk. "Janis would be happy to get it for you while we talk."

"No, thanks," Carrie said.

"I'll get a cup on my way out," Dade stated, not wanting to waste time.

"What brings you to my office?" Sheriff Sawmill took a sip and set the mug down. He picked up the packet and tore the corner. He dumped the small pill onto his palm and then popped it into his mouth, chasing it with water from a bottle on his desk.

"When I was closing my store earlier, I was cornered by one of the festival workers in the alley." Carrie crossed her legs and rocked her foot back and forth. Dade remembered her nervous tic from high school.

"Did he touch you or hurt you in any way?" The sheriff's gaze scanned Carrie as though looking for any signs of struggle.

"Not exactly." The admission seemed to make her uncomfortable, considering the way she started fidgeting.

"Threaten you?" Sheriff Sawmill leaned forward, making more tears in the corner of the empty Zantac packet.

"He backed me up against the wall but was interrupted be—"

The sheriff's desk phone rang. He glanced at the screen. "Excuse me for a minute while I take this."

Carrie nodded.

Dade could see where this was going, and regret stabbed him for dragging her here in the first place. The sheriff, his staff and the volunteers were overwhelmed. The festival worker hadn't exactly threatened Carrie—*intimidated* was a better word. Her neighbor had interceded, and then Dade had arrived on the scene. The worker had left without so much as making a threat for anyone else to hear. As frustrating and scary as this whole situation was for her, nothing illegal had happened.

The sheriff ended the call and shot them an apologetic look. "It's been a little hectic around here. Please, continue."

"I was backed up against the wall, so I got ready to use my pepper spray when Samuel Jenkins showed up and interrupted Nash," she said.

"I know the Jenkins boy," Sawmill said with a nod of acknowledgment. It didn't matter how old a man was in Cattle Barge. He would always be known by his family association. *The Jenkins boy. The Butler boy.* No matter how much Dade tried to distance himself in order to be his own man, he'd always be Maverick Mike's boy. "And Nash is…?"

"The festival worker," she clarified.

The phone rang again, and the sheriff let out a sharp sigh as he pinched the bridge of his nose. "Hold on for one second."

Dade could see this was going nowhere. He stood and Sheriff Sawmill immediately put his caller on hold.

"I'm sorry about the interruptions," Sawmill began. "We get several dozen calls a day from citizens who think someone might be following them or their crazy uncle is hatching a plan to murder them and some of those complainants have access to my direct line considering most of us have lived in this town all of our lives. We all go way back." His eyes flashed at Dade. "The town's been in a tizzy for weeks and everyone's on alert."

"We understand. We'll give a statement to one of the deputies out front." Dade waved off the sheriff.

"My office will do everything in its power to ensure the safety of its citizens." It was the line the sheriff had most likely given to every small-time complainant since his world had blown up.

When Dade really thought about their case, he couldn't argue. No real crime had been committed, and that tied the sheriff's hands. Normally, Sawmill would go talk to the offender and that was deterrent enough, but his plate was full and the festival was on its way out of town in the morning. Problem solved for Carrie.

"We'll check the festival's schedule and reach out to local law enforcement and ask to be made aware of any similar complaints."

"Thank you," Dade said as Carrie stood, seeming to catch on immediately to the underlying current. Anyone could see that the sheriff's office was being inundated, so a case like Carrie's would be swept under the rug. Not for lack of concern, but because resources were too thin and solving a high-profile murder would take precedence.

"Everyone holding up okay at the ranch?" Sawmill asked.

Dade nodded as he put his hand on the small of Carrie's back.

"Anything you can do is appreciated, Sheriff," he said, leading her toward the same hallway they'd traversed moments before with the knowledge it wouldn't be much.

THE SHERIFF'S OFFICE boomed with activity even at this late hour. Carrie was tired. She wanted to go home, wash off the day and cuddle her dog, Coco. Giving her statement to the deputy hadn't taken long, but it was getting late.

"He can't help, can he?" Carrie released her words on a sigh. This seemed like a good time to be grateful Nash would be long gone in the morning and her life would return to normal as soon as the situation with Brett calmed down.

"Doesn't appear so." Dade seemed as frustrated as she felt.

Bright lights assaulted her the second she stepped out of the air-conditioning and into the August heat. There was so much flash and camera lighting that it seemed like the sun had come out.

The swarm followed them to Dade's truck, and a couple of cars tailed them even when they got on the road, snapping pictures. It was a dangerous situation. She could certainly see why Dade had taken the alley in order to stay under the radar.

"I'm sorry the sheriff's office wasn't more help," he said. "I should've realized what the place would be like."

"There's been a crime wave in town following your dad's…" She couldn't bring herself to say the word *murder*.

"Seems most of it has been targeted toward my

family." There was an undercurrent of anger in Dade's voice.

"Have you even had a chance to process any of this?" Carrie wished there was something she could say or do. "Here you're helping me when you have so much on your plate already."

"Good to think about something besides my own problems for a change." He put on his turn signal and changed lanes. "Did you eat dinner? We could stop off."

"I wish I could." She started to apologize but he stopped her. "I have a dog that needs to go out. Her name's Coco and she's a Sharp Eagle, which is a cross between a shar-pei and a beagle. She has the beauty of a shar-pei and the sweet temperament of a beagle." Carrie realized about halfway through her monologue that she was talking too fast. Being alone in a truck with Dade shouldn't make her feel anxious, so she chalked her heightened feelings up to the crazy end of the day and not the electricity pinging through her body being this near him. "I'm talking too much."

"Where am I taking you?" Dade half grinned, one side of his mouth curling in a smile that had been cute on a boy and was sexy as hell on a grown man.

Carrie felt her cheeks burn.

"Back to my car is fine. That way I'll be able to get to work in the morning without calling in any favors." She had no idea who she'd call. Carrie had been too busy with the sweet shop to make friends. At least, that's the excuse she gave when she sat at home Friday nights after work instead of meeting pals for dinner. Her social calendar wasn't exactly full, and she still felt like that gawky teenager she'd been. The truth was that ever since she'd returned to Cattle Barge in high school after being shifted to a group home in Kilburn City, she'd felt like an outsider. But then, no other place had felt like home, either. As silly as it sounded, even to her, the last time she'd felt like she belonged somewhere was primary school in Cattle Barge. Coming back had been an attempt to recover the feeling. So far, she'd supplied the town with the best ice cream she could create—at least that was something.

Thinking about the past, about *her* past, had a way of creating instant tension in her body. A headache threatened, so she pinched the bridge of her nose.

"The ice cream shop seems to be doing well. It's all anyone can talk about." The hint of pride in Dade's voice caused ripples of hope—maybe a sense of belonging?—to bubble inside her chest.

"It's definitely been keeping me on my toes, and I'm grateful people seem to like it." The store made her feel part of the community, even if a counter stood between her and the rest of the world.

"I hear your employees like working for you," he continued, more of that pride in his voice.

"One of my business professors taught me to hire

for attitude. He said everything else can be learned."
She'd completed her associate degree at the community college in Kilgore while waitressing nights. Studying and working was about all she'd had time for in her early twenties. She couldn't deny her focus was paying off now.

"Sounds like the guy knew what he was talking about," Dade said.

"What about you?" Carrie wanted to know what had happened to Dade after high school when she'd moved away to go to college.

"I joined the service after graduation. Served my country and came home to the ranch to work the land," he said, pulling into the alley. "Not sure how long I'll stick around once the dust settles, though."

Before she could ask what that meant, a strong sense of foreboding settled on her shoulders, like a heavy blanket. But it was probably nothing, right?

Until she caught a glimpse of red on the driver's side door of her car. A single rose.

Strange. It hadn't been there earlier.

Chapter Three

"Getting a flower should be a good thing," Carrie said to Dade, who pulled alongside her sedan and parked. She shoved aside the notion that he might be planning to move away. She had no real right to ask about his personal life. "But this just feels creepy."

"I'll check it out." He hopped out of the cab.

She didn't budge. There was something safe about being with Dade, despite the media scrutiny and everything going on with her pulse. Too bad the secure feeling wouldn't last. And she needed to get home to Coco anyway.

Dade came around to her side and opened the door. "Whoever left this didn't identify himself."

He snapped a pic and said he was texting it to the sheriff.

"It's probably from Brett." He'd given her a single rose early on in their relationship.

"Either way, the sheriff needs to know," Dade quickly said.

In Brett's last voice mail—the one he'd left after he calmed down and started thinking rationally again—he'd said that he'd do pretty much anything to win her back. Was he trying to remind her of happier times? She frowned. There was no chance she was going out with him again. Her favorite pair of jogging shorts was at his place—or at least she thought so, because she couldn't find them in her house even though she could've sworn she'd worn them last weekend. Maybe she hadn't looked hard enough. In all the stress and confusion of the past couple of weeks, she was starting to lose her mind. Another reason she wished Brett could accept the breakup and move on. Being the cause of someone else's pain wasn't exactly a good feeling.

"Does this guy have a hard time understanding when a relationship is over?" An emotion—jealousy?—passed behind Dade's serious blues.

Carrie was most likely imagining it, seeing what she wanted instead of what was really there. Compassion. And sympathy? Damn. She didn't want his pity.

"Like I said, the breakup didn't go over well." With a sharp intake of air, Carrie exited the truck.

"You'll be okay?" More of that concern was present in Dade's voice.

"Yeah, fine. Thank you for taking me to the sheriff and especially for wandering down the alley when you did. I'm sorry the media has you banished to the shadows, but I can't imagine what might've happened if you hadn't been there." An involuntary shiver rocked her. She thought about Dade reporting the rose to the sheriff. It wasn't a crime to do something that many would consider a nice gesture from an ex who was most likely saying he was sorry. But after hearing about Dade's sister, she could see why he'd be overly cautious.

"Do me a favor. Park in front of the building tomorrow." Dade took a step back, like he needed more space in between them. Not exactly a reassuring move.

"No question there," she responded, dodging eye contact. As it was, electricity hummed through her body being this close to Dade. If only she'd felt this way about Brett, things would've turned out differently. Brett wasn't Dade. The two couldn't be more different. Dade was serious and could be intense, but there was something comfortable and magnetic about being with him. Brett rode a motorcycle and had an edge to his personality, and that had been the initial draw. He was so completely different than her, than anyone she'd dated in the past. Maybe a little bit dangerous, too. Looking back, he was more show than substance, which was one of many reasons she'd walked away before the relationship became too serious.

Brett liked to consider himself a thrill seeker, thus the motorcycle and the biker attitude. Real danger was deploying halfway across the world to face a foreign enemy in order to protect an ideal—freedom—

not riding around in a leather jacket looking for a fistfight.

"Do you want me to take care of this?" Dade nodded toward the flower dangling from his hand at his side.

"Would you mind? I don't want to deal with it right now." She made a huge mistake in glancing up. Sensual shivers skittered across her exposed skin. She could admit to being embarrassed that she'd been blind enough to get into a bad relationship. She could blame her lapse in judgment on a million things, not the least of which would be working long hours to get her business off the ground. But the truth was that she'd been lonely. Brett was good-looking and charming when he needed to be—especially in the beginning. He'd seemed so proud of her at first, but then it had turned into something else, something possessive. She'd lost interest, and he wasn't taking it so well. "I must seem like a complete idiot for not seeing this coming."

"In my experience, people don't always show their true colors until you really get to know them. That takes time," he said after a thoughtful pause, and she figured there was a bigger story behind those words. "You have good judgment, Carrie. You always were smarter than the rest of us. Everyone makes mistakes now and then. Don't be too hard on yourself."

His reassuring words calmed her. She shouldn't allow them to. She knew better than to let herself depend on anyone else. Carrie had learned early in life that all people let her down eventually, from addict parents she'd never met to a system that put her in the hands of an abuser to a distant aunt who'd claimed Carrie and then dumped her back in the system when it became inconvenient to keep her.

Where'd that come from?

This night and the reunion were taking a toll, and she needed to get her emotions in check.

"Stop by the shop sometime," she said. "Dessert is on the house."

Dade cracked a smile. "Guess there are perks to knowing the owner."

"The first treat is for old times' sake. You're on your own from there," she quipped, thinking how nice it was not to have to work at conversation for a change. It had always been like that with Dade. Easy. Light. Fun. *When we were young*, she corrected. High school had been another matter altogether.

Things changed. And so did people.

The serious blue eyes Dade had possessed as a child were even more intense now. As easy as conversation had been between them all those years ago, neither had spoken about their demons—demons that grew and changed people over time. Demons that could make a man sign up to travel halfway around the world to fight a monster he couldn't see.

The two chatted easily for another fifteen minutes, catching up on more of each other's lives in the past few years.

"It's good seeing you again, Dade," she said, finally looking up and realizing what a mistake that was. Because he was looking, too. And the way he was looking made her body ache in a way it hadn't in far too long.

"You, too, Carrie."

Neither made a move to leave right away. Another mistake. They were racking up. Because she'd learned early on that feelings could trick her. All she was experiencing was a bout of nostalgia. She'd taken psychology as an elective to help sort out her own emotions. Dade represented the past—a time before life became confusing and people who were supposed to take care of her had hurt her. A time before the group home leader had snapped and taken out his frustrations on her and a handful of other kids. A time before she'd been placed in a foster home with a real monster and had a social worker who seemed content to look the other way in order to check a box on a file—*placed*.

"I better get home to Coco."

"The Sharp Eagle?" The corner of his mouth lifted in a grin that tugged at her heart.

She laughed despite all the memories churning through her mind.

"Yep." She returned the smile. "Like I said, stop by some time."

Neither seemed ready to leave, but it was time,

so she made the first move, digging her keys out of her purse. She palmed the pepper spray.

"Keep that ready to go just in case." Dade's eyes went straight to the palm-sized black canister in the leather casing as he stepped aside to allow passage.

"I will." She took the first step toward her vehicle, grateful the rose had been removed from the driver's-side door handle. Brett's timing couldn't be worse. But then, timing wasn't his only issue.

"Hold on to it even when you walk the dog. Madelyn had a restraining order against her ex, and it didn't stop him from coming after her." His warning sent a cold chill down her back. He was right. She'd read about the whole ordeal in the news and, even though she thought she knew Brett, Dade's half sister must've felt the same about her boyfriend.

Dade fished a card out of his wallet and handed it to her. "The sheriff's office might be too busy to handle this properly, but if this guy shows up again or your ex doesn't take the hint and you need a hand, give me a call. My personal cell's on there."

"Thank you." She dropped his card in her purse. Nash should be gone by morning. She hoped Brett would leave things alone. Experience had taught her that he didn't give up so easily. But she could handle him. Right?

As Dade watched Carrie drive away, regret filled his chest. Since that was as productive as drinking well water next to a nuclear facility, he started the engine of his truck and navigated out of the alley.

Dade spent the half-hour ride home lost in his thoughts, one of which hadn't dawned on him until later. Being close to Carrie might bring unwanted media attention to her and dredge up her past. People talked. He'd never been truly sure what had happened to her in the years she was away from Cattle Barge, but she'd returned a different person. The chatty and sweet girl from their youth had seemed... he didn't know...lost?

Adding to his sharp mood was the simple fact that his own life was a mess. First, there'd been an unexpected breakup with his girlfriend, followed by the Mav's murder and everything that had happened to the family since. Going back to the ranch didn't hold a hell of a lot of appeal lately, but he had nowhere else to be and was needed at home. He was restless, though. Working the land was the only activity that had ever given him a sense of peace. The Mav had been right about one thing—hard work made for clear focus right up until Dade came in from the range. Honestly, focus had been hard to come by lately, but he figured he could get it back if he kept moving forward. Was it the fact that someone had murdered his father right under their noses in such a violent fashion and on the land they all loved so much that kept him on edge?

Going to bed would be useless. Sleep was as close

as Helsinki to Houston. He made a beeline for the kitchen after parking in his usual spot. The light was on, and six weeks ago that might've seemed odd. Nothing surprised him now.

"Did you just pull in?" Ella seemed happy for the first time, but then Dade's older sister had gotten the closure she needed from the past. She'd also met a man she truly seemed in love with, and while Dade was happy for his sister, seeing her in that state of bliss reminded him just how far away he was from it. He wouldn't begrudge her, though. She deserved every bit of it.

"Got sidetracked on my way to pick up the bronze." Dade realized that he'd never made it over to the mayor's office.

"I figured as much after Mayor Bentley called. Dalton volunteered to go instead." She sat at the long wooden table behind a bowl of ice cream. "Everything okay?"

"Yeah." He'd thank his twin brother when he saw him in the morning. Days on the ranch began at 4:00 a.m., so that wouldn't be long. Dade went for the coffeepot, figuring a caffeine boost would help him think clearly. After seeing Carrie again, his mind was going to a place he knew better than to let it: an inappropriate attraction that had him remembering the lines of her heart-shaped face framed by inky-black hair, her creamy skin, smooth aside from that little scar to the left side of her full lips. When she smiled, she had one dimple on her left cheek, and part of him wanted to see that again.

"We're out of beans in the kitchen." Ella nodded toward the pantry.

"Since when is this house out of anything?" There'd been someone around to stock the pantry and make sure meals were cooked and the kids put to bed for as long as Dade could remember. None of the good people providing those tasks had been his parents.

"I'm sure there's more somewhere. May's been overworked, and I thought she should take it easy. I asked her to take a couple of days for herself."

Dade almost laughed out loud. May, take a break? She wasn't the lounging type. "How'd that go over?"

Ella looked at him. "It'll be worse if she realizes we wanted something and had to do without."

"Why would we do that? I'll check dry storage to see if we have a can of coffee hiding in there. She'll never know. Besides, we're all grown. We can do for ourselves." She would take it to heart. Feel like she'd let them down in some way. It was just coffee, but May wouldn't see it that way. May had always done everything for them when they were kids. May was a saint.

"Where were you tonight?" Ella had taken to prying in everyone's business since their father's murder and the subsequent crimes against the family.

"There was a disturbance in town and I got distracted." He searched for pain relievers to stem the dull headache focused in the center of his forehead.

"What happened? Are you okay?" There was so much worry in her voice now. The reason was understandable, but Dade could take care of himself.

"Nothing that involved me directly. I helped a friend," he conceded, taking a seat across from Ella.

"You're sure about that?" Fear widened her eyes.

"Certain. Carrie Palmer had a run-in with a festival worker. I took her to file a complaint." The world would know tomorrow anyway. There was no sense in hiding it.

Ella glanced at her bowl of ice cream and started to speak.

"Have you heard from Cadence?" He changed the subject, not yet ready to discuss Carrie with his sister. Hell, he wasn't sure what he was feeling toward her other than a strong urge to protect her.

"She's still down with the flu and, honestly, with everything going on around here, it's probably best she's out of town until the hysteria dies down." Ella pushed around the ball of ice cream in her bowl.

"What she did to Madelyn was inexcusable—"

Ella was already nodding in agreement. Leaving a threatening message to try to force Madelyn out of town was a low blow. "Our baby sister messed up. I'm just grateful Madelyn has found it in her heart to forgive Cadence. Their relationship still has a long way to go but they're making progress, talking almost every day."

"I'm guessing their reconciliation has a lot to do with you," Dade pointed out.

"With everything this family has been through we need each other now more than ever." Ella's heart was always big and her judgment sound.

"There's no rush for me but Ed can't read Dad's will until we're all present. He also said the date's been set," Dade informed. Ed Staples was the family's lawyer and longtime friend of their father. Some people might say that Ed was Maverick Mike's only true confidant.

"Ed told me, too." Ella rolled the spoon through her ice cream.

He eyed the label. It came from Carrie's Cold Treats.

"Ed said there was some kind of stipulation." Dade didn't care a hill of beans about what he stood to inherit. The only reason he cared about the will was because there might be a revelation in it that could blow open the investigation and bring their father's killer to justice. It sat hard on his chest that his father had been murdered on the ranch, that someone had had access and had wanted to prove they could do whatever they wanted at Maverick Mike's home. What did that say about security? About Dade and his brother? Early on, folks had speculated that Andrea Caldwell, the Mav's girlfriend, had shot him in his sleep. Dade hadn't taken the rumor seriously.

Andrea was a sweet person. She might not be able to take care of herself but she wouldn't hurt a fly. It wasn't her nature.

"Wish I knew what he was talking about," Ella admitted. "Do you?"

"Guess we'll learn together." Dade filled a water glass and drained it. "When does Holden get here?"

"A couple of days," she said, her eyes getting a little spark in them when she referred to her fiancé. "He's closing out his accounts in Virginia so he can move here. I wanted to go with him, but he thought I'd feel better if I stayed on the ranch while everything's been so crazy."

"He's probably right," Dade agreed.

Ella stood, moved to the sink and rinsed out her bowl before placing it in the dishwasher. "Guess my eyes were bigger than my stomach."

"I'll see you in the morning," Dade said. By the time he returned to the kitchen with a can of ground coffee, Ella had gone to bed. It was late. A shower and the idea of sleep won out over making coffee.

After climbing in bed, Dade drew the covers up. His mind drifted to the last gift from his father, a fishing rod. Not just any fishing rod, but the one he'd wanted as a kid. There'd been a note, too. One that Dade had balled up and tossed into a drawer without reading. He'd been filled with anger and figured one small gesture couldn't wipe away the abuse Dade had suffered at his father's hands. Now he'd never have another chance to make things right with the old man. To add insult to injury, the note had gone missing.

The sheriff was no closer to making an arrest now than he'd been a week ago. There were too many leads and too many distractions between the media and others who'd descended on Cattle Barge. Claims of paternity or debts owed from Maverick Mike were through the roof. Only one paternity claim had panned out so far, and Madelyn Kensington had arrived at the ranch seeming even less thrilled with the news than the Butlers had been.

Rather than chew on those unproductive nuggets, Dade flipped onto his back. He'd been in bed long enough for his eyes to adjust to the dark, so he stared up at the ceiling, at the texture he'd heard his sisters describe as orange peel. The pattern stretched from wall to wall.

Out of nowhere, Dade felt hemmed in. He used to love having his own wing in the main house, but now it felt like a cage.

Tonight must be the night for fruitless thoughts, because his mind turned to Carrie and how good it had been to see her again. He told himself it was her safety that had him wanting to check on her in the morning when he had work to do.

What time did her sweet shop open? He picked up his phone on the nightstand and glanced at the time. One o'clock in the morning. Work started in three hours. He thumbed the internet icon and then entered the name of her shop.

She opened at eleven o'clock, which meant she probably arrived by seven or eight to prep for the day.

The festival worker should be long gone by then. Shouldn't he? It was probably the brush with death two of his sisters had had recently that had Dade's mind twisting over his thoughts, concerned about Carrie.

Because what if Nash had left that rose? What did that say about the man's intentions?

Chapter Four

"Coco, come here, girl." Carrie glanced around the backyard of her one-story bungalow, looking for her dog. Normally, she liked living in a suburb on the edge of the small town with its cul-de-sacs and third-of-an-acre lots. Tonight, she looked out into the blackness with apprehension. Was it always this dark outside on a weeknight? All the homes on her street were blacked out, and no one seemed to see the need to waste electricity by leaving a porch light on.

This had never bothered her before, but Nash had caught her off guard, setting her nerves even more on edge after dealing with Brett. Where was her dog?

Carrie stepped onto the back porch and called for Coco again. Her dog had run around the side of the house, which wasn't unusual, but Carrie didn't like it tonight. Out of habit, she'd dropped her keys next to the front door, along with her pepper spray. All kinds of worrisome thoughts plagued her. Technically, the festival wouldn't pack up and leave until morning. Could Nash have figured out where she lived? He might've followed her home one evening. No. She would've known. She would've noticed an unfamiliar car or truck.

"Coco," she repeated, louder this time. And then she listened for the sounds of the dog tags clanking together—the proof of rabies vaccination always jingled when she moved. All she could hear were cicadas and crickets, which sounded haunting tonight. Keep thinking along those lines and she'd really psych herself out. Okay, it was too late for that. *It'll be fine, Carrie.*

Glancing into the shadows, a prickly sensation that someone was watching overtook her. This time she studied the dark corners of her yard. The glow from the back porch lit up barely more than her deck. Again, she asked herself if Nash could've followed her home. No way. She and Dade had talked for a long time after the encounter and they'd gone to the sheriff's office. Her nerves were fried, and what she really needed was a cool shower, a good meal and sleep. It was time to put this awful day to rest and wake with a clean slate tomorrow.

The sound of a truck engine hummed from down the street. As the noise moved toward her, she whistled for her dog and made kissing noises. Those usually did the trick. Not tonight.

Carrie took a couple of steps back, placing her hand on the doorknob leading into the kitchen. As soon as Coco darted onto the deck, Carrie would be ready to usher her baby inside and quickly lock the door behind them. Why did her dog always exert her independence at the worst possible times?

Gravel crunched underneath tires as her neighbor's truck engine roared and then died. The bungalow next door had been rented six months ago by a single guy who seemed intent on keeping to himself. After several fruitless attempts to stop by and introduce herself, Carrie wondered if he wanted to be on friendly terms at all. Tonight probably wasn't the best time for a conversation and since he'd made no effort so far, she figured he might be a jerk anyway. He kept odd hours, even to her, and she hadn't seen him outside since he moved in. He was gone for days at a time with no indication of where he'd been. Lights in his house were on at odd times. Carrie had noticed them when Coco was sick and needed to go outside during the night. He never had company—or at least he didn't while she'd been home. She could admit that wasn't often since she'd opened the sweet shop last year.

"Your trash keeps blowing into my yard," an irritated male voice snapped. That was a nice introduction. He must've seen her in the porch light. She sure as heck couldn't see him, and the thought sent an icy chill racing up her arms.

"Sorry. It's the raccoons. I work long hours at—"

The truck's door slammed a little too loudly, causing her to jump. *Take it easy, buddy.*

"Lock it up." His voice was almost a growl.

If he was going to be this much of a jerk, she saw no point in introducing herself or trying to make nice, so she didn't respond at all.

A few seconds later, she saw a light flip on inside his house. Guess he'd made his neighborly intentions clear. She blew out a breath. This had been one red-letter day for sure.

Coco's tags jingled, and relief washed over Carrie as her little dog bolted into view, barking. Instead of hopping onto the deck, Coco diverted right and ran in a circle as fast as she could, disappearing into the shadows only to dart back inside the light. Her barks intensified with each sighting. Her reaction came a little too late to have an impact on Jerk Face. Coco was a sweetheart, but her neighbor didn't have to know that, and she could sound menacing when she really wanted to. She looked more like a shar-pei than a beagle, which made her a little more threatening.

Even though Carrie was starving, she stood on the porch a few more minutes, almost daring her neighbor to come out and say something again about the noise. Her dog had been inside since lunch. She needed a little freedom, and Carrie was finding her bravado again after the encounter with Jerk Face. She didn't have enough audacity to walk out front and check the mail, she thought, realizing she'd forgotten to do that on the drive in. It could wait. No way was she walking out the front door in the dark and to the middle of the cul-de-sac, where all the mailboxes were clumped together to make it easier on the mail carrier.

There were four houses to each cul-de-sac in this neighborhood and hers sat directly across from the Hardin place. Marla Hardin was Samuel's aging aunt and he lived there with her.

Humidity filled the air, and the promise of a rare August rain hung low and heavy. Shiny white stars cut through the pitch-black canopy overhead.

Coco finally conceded her playtime was over and hopped onto the deck. Her tongue hung out one side of her mouth as she panted. She had the snout of a shar-pei—it wasn't exactly created to thrive in the heat.

"Are you ready, sweet girl?" Carrie bent down and scratched her dog behind the ears. The eerie feeling of being watched crept over her, so she made kissing noises at Coco before scooting inside. She closed and locked the door behind them. Her purse hung off a chair in the eat-in kitchen, and she noticed crumbs on the floor underneath it. She'd mopped the floor before work, which meant that Coco must've dug into the garbage again.

She scooped them up. Odd. They had a distinct smell…like the ham-flavored training treats Carrie had stopped buying when the vet had said Coco was tipping the scale. Carrie thought she'd thrown them all out, but she must've forgotten a bag in her pantry. She glanced around, the eerie feeling returning. She thought about the pepper spray attached to her key ring on the credenza by the front door and decided to sleep with it next to the bed. The incident with Nash had really thrown her off-balance—that must be why she felt on pins and needles in her own home.

Coco followed on Carrie's heels as she double-checked all the doors to make sure they were locked. She took a quick shower, ate a bowl of cereal and then climbed into bed. She'd always considered Cattle Barge a safe place to live in general, and especially after the horrors she'd endured when she was taken away. She'd never really thought about being a single woman living on her own and working long hours at the treat shop until now.

Between Brett, Nash and her unfriendly, keep-to-himself Jerk Face neighbor, she figured it wouldn't hurt to look into having a security system installed. Coco provided some insurance against a surprise predator. She usually barked at strangers. But after Coco's lackluster performance with the neighbor, Carrie decided her backup needed backup. Even so, with her dog curled up at the foot of the bed, warming her legs, Carrie felt a little safer. Unless someone tossed a piece of meat onto the floor, Carrie thought with an almost smile.

The next morning, she woke to the sound of Coco

growling. Her dog was at the doorway to the bedroom, starting down the hallway. Carrie grabbed the small canister of pepper spray off the nightstand and threw the covers off.

Coco wasted no time darting toward the noise. Carrie couldn't hear much of anything over the barking, but all she could think was *so Jerk Face neighbor gets a free pass but the UPS guy is suspect?*

It was the UPS guy, right?

She followed her dog to the front door, checking out the window for the brown van. To be fair, this was the same reaction Coco had to the postal worker and the guy who'd tried to deliver flowers once. Amazon delivered to her door, but she didn't remember ordering anything online. Then again, she'd been busy, working extra hours since the festival, and sometimes she entered her home address when she meant to use the sweet shop's.

Speaking of which, Nash should be packed up and out of town this morning. That was a relief. Too bad he couldn't take Brett with him, she thought with another almost smile.

Coco was doing her mix of bark-howling, which had been so cute when she was a three-month-old pup. Not so much at a year.

There was no way Carrie was opening the door until she could confirm who was out there. She stroked her dog's head, thinking Coco must've heard a squirrel. Wouldn't be the first time this had happened. "It's okay, girl."

After double-checking and being perfectly satisfied nothing was going on, Carrie opened the door. A stuffed animal lay at her feet. She picked up the black-and-white orca whale. *Brett*.

She scanned the front yard. There were kids riding bikes around the cul-de-sac, and that was about it.

"Okay, puppy. Way to keep me safe from the neighborhood children. Let's get back inside." Brett was the only one who knew whales were her favorite. She checked her phone and found several texts from him. They'd be more apologies. More of him being frustrated that she wasn't returning his calls. She'd deal with those and with him later. Now, she needed coffee.

Carrie walked by the trash can in the kitchen and tossed the awkward gift on top. *Take a hint, buddy*.

An hour later, she parked under a tree in the lot of the strip shopping center. The rain never came last night, so the air was still thick with humidity. She noticed the festival trucks were still there. Everything was packed up and looked ready to go across the street in the lot of Ventnor's Park. *Not another day of Nash*, she thought with a groan. Going to the sheriff last night seemed like an even better idea this morning. A complaint was on record. If Nash irritated her, she had every intention of telling him she'd reported him.

The icy chill returned—it was becoming a little too familiar.

Focusing on her morning routine at the store kept her distracted. Carrie liked to be the first one in the shop. She could prepare the bank deposit and relock it inside the safe before anyone showed up for work. That way she could deal with money so her employees wouldn't even have to know where it was kept. Protecting her employees was always at the top of her priority list.

Harper Stoddard was the first to arrive. The nineteen-year-old's cell was in her hand, and as soon as she looked up at Carrie, her brown eyes widened. "Everything okay?"

"Peachy. We need to cover a few things when Eric shows, but I'd rather wait until the both of you are here before we talk about last night."

Harper walked over to Carrie and embraced her. "I'm just glad you're all right."

How did she know something had happened? Then it dawned on Carrie that being seen with Dade Butler would be news. Social media seemed to keep people constantly in the know. "Me, too. We'll put some controls in place to make sure you and Eric don't run into any problems."

"I'm not worried about us. You always make sure we're covered. I'm concerned about you." Harper had a point. Carrie always made sure her employees left together, while she locked up alone most nights.

"I'll be more careful." Harper's thoughtfulness touched Carrie deeply.

Eric, her assistant manager, arrived, breaking into the emotional moment. Harper excused herself.

"Everything all right with you this morning, boss?" he asked as Harper opened the freezer to bring out tubs of ice cream to stock the front bins.

Carrie acknowledged Eric's frown. He must've heard the news as well, judging by the concern written in his intense expression.

She deflected the sudden burst of emotion springing tears to her eyes by saying, "That was nothing. Coco kept me up barking last night."

But her employees' genuine concern touched her in a deep place.

"That stinks." Harper flashed her eyes at Carrie. "Puppies can be so much work."

"What time did you get in this morning?" Eric asked, motioning toward the fresh rack of waffle cones.

"Early." Carrie followed Harper into the fridge, picking up a heavy container of Vanilla Bean-illa, a Carrie's Cold Treats favorite. She'd set up several trays of baked goods in the front counter and signed on to the cash register. She needed to figure out the best way to discuss last night with her employees.

"In early after staying late last night?" Eric moved beside Carrie. "Let me help with that."

"I got it."

Overseeing every detail of Carrie's Cold Treats had been her passion—the shop was her passion. And a little voice reminded her that she didn't have much else, considering she lived in a rented house. Coco was a bright spot, but her pup was a little short on conversation.

Fresh from a breakup, dating was out of the question at the moment. Maybe she needed to step out of her comfort zone and share her pet project a little more. The last thing she wanted was for her employees to feel like she didn't trust them. Eric was a nice guy, a strong assistant manager who was working to put himself through the local satellite campus of the University of Texas.

"I could be better about sharing some of the load, and I have complete trust in both of you to do a good job." She handed over the tray as a knock sounded at the back door. Fear caused her to freeze, because for a split second she thought it might be Nash returning to finish what had been interrupted last night. The thought was irrational, and yet it had her pulse pounding anyway. The festival trucks had not pulled away yet as she'd hoped they would've done by now.

"I got this," Eric said.

She wouldn't argue. She deposited the freezing-cold tub into the front bin and walked toward her office, figuring it was most likely a delivery.

Teddy Ginger, her milk delivery driver, waltzed in and stopped at her office door with one of those cheesy used-car-salesman smiles. He was a little taller than her and lanky. Teddy had a ruddy complexion and beady blue eyes. He was midthirties and on the thin side. "How's business?" Teddy was always good for a smile and a joke.

"Good. Thanks for asking. I have your check right here." She held up the offering, standing on the opposite side of the glass desk.

Teddy reached out for it. "Thank you much."

"Cooler's open, so feel free to load up," she said, softening her expression.

"I'll be out of your way in a jiff," Teddy replied. He made quick work of delivering his product.

"Have a good weekend, Teddy."

"Same to you." Teddy waved as he wheeled out his dolly.

"I see we already have a customer waiting for us to open." Harper motioned toward the front of the store. Plexiglas made up half of her office wall. She'd had it constructed that way so that she could be in her office while keeping an eye on business in case one of her employees needed help at the counter.

Carrie glanced at the clock. Five minutes until opening. She looked at the front window. *Samuel?*

"I know him. He's not really a customer. He's most likely checking on me after what happened last night."

"And what was that exactly?" Eric whirled around to face Carrie as she walked up.

"I thought you already knew," she said.

"We'd like to hear it directly from you. I mean, you can't always trust what people say." Harper motioned toward the phone she kept in her apron pocket.

Carrie needed to explain the situation without scaring them.

"I had a weird run-in last night with a festival worker in the alley." Carrie regretted her shaky tone. She didn't really want to go into the details but realized her employees had a right to know, for safety's sake.

"What happened?" Harper asked.

"It was probably nothing, but I filed a report with the sheriff as a precaution. From now on make sure you park in front of the building." Carrie's attempt to lighten her tone didn't have the intended effect. Instead she sounded even more strained. She cleared her throat. "To be on the safe side."

"Was it the guy who kept coming in here loitering?" Eric's gaze intensified.

Carrie nodded.

"I knew I should've stayed late and walked you out." Eric had enough on his plate between summer school and work without worrying about her.

"It's fine. There were people around, and I got

lucky that Samuel and an old friend of mine happened to be walking through the alley. I had all the backup I needed." She appreciated the thought, though, and the concern. "But I don't want either of you closing the shop on your own. From now on, we double-team everything." It might cost a little more to have two employees stay until closing, but the money was worth it to guarantee their safety. Besides, business had been good. The shop had gotten into the black sooner than she'd expected. Having something she created take off so well brought an enormous sense of accomplishment and security to Carrie. She would do whatever was necessary in order to protect what she'd created from scratch. "Buddy system from here on out."

She walked toward the door. She unlocked it and turned the open sign over. "And, I'll probably start bringing Coco in with me again if I get in a position to close by myself."

"We'll make sure that doesn't happen but we like having Coco around." Eric seemed to accept that answer.

Samuel looked pasty and nervous, like he was still shaken from the encounter with Nash last night. Carrie turned to Harper before opening the door and motioned toward the register. "Might as well open up and get business flowing. It'll be hard to top this week's sales, though."

She smiled at Samuel while scanning the parking

lot looking for signs of Nash. Across the street she could clearly see the line of festival trucks parked there. That sensation of being watched had returned, and a creepy-crawly feeling sent chilly tingles up her spine. Too bad the caravan was still across the street. Not one truck had moved.

"Come on in, Samuel. I owe you an ice cream."

DADE HAD BEEN working for seven hours by the time Carrie opened her sweet shop. He'd been distracted today. He blamed lack of sleep, but the truth was that he kept thinking about running into Carrie again after so many years. And he wanted to see to it that she was all right after last night. She'd been on his mind since he'd returned to Cattle Barge and had learned that she'd opened a shop downtown.

"Remind me later that I have to get an emergency delivery of hay for the horses when we head inside. We won't last another day with the feed we have on hand," Dade's twin brother, Dalton, said.

"I'll pick it up in town." A visit to the feed store would be as good excuse as any to pop into town. He could drop in to collect that cold treat from Carrie while he was at it.

His twin brother shot him a look.

"It's on my way," Dade hedged, needing a minute to come up with a plausible excuse. He and Dalton had always been close, and his brother could read him a little too easily.

"Why do you need to go into town again?" Dalton's brow arched.

"The Olsen widow has something for May. Figured I'd save her a trip if she hasn't picked it up yet. Ella thinks May's been working too hard since the funeral." Dade had no plans to share that he really wanted to check on Carrie.

Dalton's brow hiked up, but he didn't say anything.

"Since when do you care why I need to run into town?" Dade deflected.

His brother shrugged. "Guess we're all acting a little different since the Mav's..."

Dalton didn't finish his sentence—didn't need to. The air at the ranch had been thick with tension ever since their father's murder. Neither of them ever discussed the man, the past.

Dade didn't want to make small talk when he could be in the shower cleaning up before heading into town. He turned his horse, Flame, toward the barn. He'd been named as a nod to his fiery chestnut coat. "I better head out before May overdoes it again and wears herself out."

"Nice of you to think of her." Dalton's eyebrow was raised, but to his credit he left it alone. "See you at supper?"

"Maybe." Being around the family, carrying on traditions held little appeal for Dade since retiring from the military to take his position on the ranch.

He loved the land and his brother and sisters, but being home was complicated and his feelings were all over the map since the murder. "How about fishing on Sunday instead?"

"Deal." Dalton seemed satisfied. His brother's concern came from a good place, and Dade appreciated the sentiment. He really wasn't trying to be a jerk. He needed space. And besides, he couldn't talk about what he didn't completely understand himself—his relationship with the Mav.

In half an hour, he was showered and on the road into town, grateful to be putting the ranch in the rearview. There was still plenty to do when he got back. Modern ranching involved patience, laptops and near-constant logging of herds. At least the recent herd of calves had sold well at auction this summer. Focusing on work had provided a good distraction in the past couple of days. But Dade didn't want to think about ranch business now. His thoughts kept bouncing back to Carrie.

By the time he made it to her shop, there was a line out the door. There was nothing like August sunshine to make folks want ice cream. He could see that the festival caravan was still parked in the lot across the street. As much as he didn't like it, there wasn't much he could do about Nash being around. The man would disappear soon enough.

Dade squinted against the sun as he strolled through the parking lot, telling himself all he was doing was checking on a friend. He considered it good news that she hadn't used the number he'd given her last night, but a tinge of regret pierced him anyway, because he liked seeing her again more than he wanted to admit.

Carrie was a strong, capable woman, and he figured there wasn't much she needed from him or anyone else. But she'd seemed rattled, and he wanted to see for himself that she was okay today first thing after she opened.

Since there was a line and she would be busy, he planned to stick his head inside the door and leave it at that.

There was a commotion going on inside the shop and…*shouting*?

Dade bolted toward the noise. His hands fisted at his sides. Carrie's voice raised above the sounds.

He listened carefully.

A shrill cry pierced his ears.

Chapter Five

"I already said I didn't leave a flower on your car, and you still haven't explained what you were doing with another dude last night." Brett's shouting caused a stir inside Carrie's shop. People scattered and mothers hid their children behind them. A couple of mothers raced toward the door, children in tow.

"I don't believe you, Brett." His iron grip on her arm had caused her to cry out in pain once already. She jerked her arm free. "You're hurting me."

The line at the counter took a couple of steps back.

"Everything's under control, folks. Mrs. Banner, bring Elsa over here. Harper will take care of both of you." Other than embarrassing Carrie, which he was, Brett was also frightening customers and her employees. And that was aggravating. Carrie had worked too hard to build her shop into the success it was becoming for one person to trample all over her sacrifices.

"Keep your voice down," she warned Brett. Carrie moved to the opposite side of the shop, far away from where Harper was handling a scared-looking Mrs. Banner.

"You need to listen," he continued, stalking around the side of the counter.

"We can talk in my office." Carrie turned, but Brett clasped her arm again. Eric, who had been watching the exchange, made a step toward them.

"It's okay," she said to Eric, peeling Brett's fingers off her. "He's not going to do anything he'll regret."

With that, she shot a warning look toward Brett.

"If you'd return my calls, it wouldn't be like this," Brett accused. Did he really believe any of this was her fault?

Wow. That was a choice.

"Keep it up and I'll call the sheriff," she muttered under her breath before turning her attention back to Eric. She motioned toward the customer who was waiting for him to retrieve her waffle cone. "Take care of Mrs. Whittle. I can handle this situation."

"How hard is it to answer when I call?" Brett demanded. Harper's shoulders tensed when Brett slammed his fist against the wall. "Or are you see-ing someone else?"

Carrie needed to get him out of the shop and away from her customers.

"Let's talk about this outside." Carrie pushed past him as the door opened and the bell jingled. She glanced up. *Dade?*

Embarrassment flamed her cheeks, thinking he was about to come face-to-face with one of her biggest mistakes. She told herself that she'd have that reaction no matter who walked through the door, but a little piece of her brain protested the lie. Her bad choice being paraded in front of the one person she really wanted to impress was the worst feeling and shrank her other accomplishments to zero.

The shop hadn't been open twenty minutes and it felt like all hell was breaking loose.

"What are you doing here, Dade?" She tried to sound calm, but her heart raced inside her chest. Brett caught up to her, anger radiating from his five-foot-ten-inch frame, so she didn't wait for Dade's response. Instead, she turned to Harper. "Can you take care of my friend? He did a huge favor for me last night and I promised him dessert on the house."

"Who's this guy?" Brett gripped her elbow possessively, his fingers digging in harder this time.

She took in a fortifying breath, not wanting to cause an even bigger scene in her place of business or in front of her friend. "Not now."

"When, Carrie? You don't talk to me anymore. You're not returning my texts or calls." Brett clamped harder. "You start accusing me of leaving stuff on your car and then this guy shows up."

"Then maybe you should take a hint and leave her alone," Dade ground out. A muscle in his jaw ticked, and his blue eyes glared a warning at Brett. She couldn't help but wince as she sidestepped Brett's grasp, praying Dade would let this go.

Brett had no idea what he was getting himself into.

"Thank you, Dade," Carrie said, trying to keep the peace in front of her customers. There were already too many side glances coming her way. "The Vanilla Bean-illa is amazing on the waffle cone dipped in chocolate. I highly recommend it."

"Sounds like the breakfast of champions, but I'll wait until the line dies down." Dade motioned toward the door.

"Things are a little hectic right now. Give me a minute. I'd like to thank you for last night."

Well, that really set Brett off. He started to say something, but seemed to think better of it when Dade's lips thinned and anger pulsed from him.

"I'll be back after I speak to my friend," she said with a glance toward Brett.

"Do you need help talking?" Dade asked, his gaze firing warning shots at her ex.

Carrie couldn't hold back a smirk. "I got this."

Brett seemed to shrink in Dade's presence, and she couldn't help but enjoy seeing him cower a little bit. He'd been a bully so far and deserved to be backed down. She would've preferred that he listened to her, but this worked, too.

"Let me know if that changes." He winked, and she should ignore all the butterflies fluttering in her stomach. Dade was being kind by stopping by. It meant nothing more to him, and she needed to keep her own emotions in check. Besides, his life was in chaos right now. It was most likely easier to think about helping someone else. He probably just needed a break from the media and being on the ranch. And speaking of complications, she made a note to herself to remember to drop off a gallon of Samuel's aunt's favorite ice cream on the way home from work. She hadn't seen the woman around lately and meant to ask Samuel if everything was okay. He was a quiet person to begin with, and his aunt did all the talking on the few occasions she'd stopped by the shop. Carrie hadn't seen Ms. Hardin in a while. Days? A week? Carrie wasn't sure.

"Will do." She led Brett outside, away from the gawking line of people and toward the trees. The August heat came at her from all angles—the sun above, the pavement below and even the breeze was hot. Typical August in Texas. It might take a while, but the weather would eventually change. *Like everything*, she thought as she spun around to face Brett. Heat radiated off him, too, in the form of anger and impatience…and possessiveness. He didn't own her and she didn't owe him an explanation for being with Dade last night.

Could her association with any crime, victim or not, impact her business? She wanted to say the idea was crazy. Reality was writing a different story.

Panic gripped her. She could not lose the one good thing in her life.

"I already told you that I needed time away from *this*." She jerked her arm free from Brett's grasp. "And what you're doing right now isn't helping your case."

"What you really mean is *us*," he ground out, and she could see that he was working himself up.

"Okay. Yes. I don't want to be together right now." She wasn't used to fighting for her own needs. The last foster home had trained that out of her. "Why don't you give me a chance to miss us?"

His anger softened to frustration, and she thought she might be making progress until his gaze narrowed and his hands fisted.

"You're not giving us a chance." The fire was back in his eyes.

The movie theater at the end of the strip mall was letting out, and a line of people spilled into the parking lot. This was probably not the best time to tell Brett he had no chance, especially with the way he'd been behaving since the breakup. He needed a couple of weeks to cool down and then they could have the conversation that had been brewing inside her for weeks.

"I don't want to hurt you. But give me a chance to think about what I want. You already know how many hours I work—"

"I backed off before and look where that got me."

He'd been more and more demanding that she spend time with him in those last few weeks, and she'd pushed back at every step.

"You have to stop texting me every five minutes and leaving gifts at my house..." Before she could finish her sentence, he threw his hands into the air and walked a tight circle.

"Then what? What is it, Carrie? Because I don't have to think about whether or not I want to spend time with you." Anger radiated off him as he smacked his fisted hand against his other palm.

Nothing good could come of such heightened emotion. She hoped she could ease him down. The idea of causing another person pain didn't sit well, yet he wasn't giving her another out. She'd been through enough hurt in one lifetime and hated the idea of causing that horrible feeling in someone else.

Carrie took in a slow deep breath, trying to keep her emotions in check. On the one hand, false hope was bad. On the other, everyone was staring at them, and this whole scenario was escalating. She was losing patience and Brett was on the verge of just losing it completely.

Brett hadn't been this interested in her when they'd been together, and she figured half of his fixation on her now had to do with her rejection. If he'd been the one to do it, he wouldn't think twice. Being on the receiving end didn't feel nice, and that's why he wanted this to work out so badly.

"What if you decide to move on while we're on a break?" He brought his hand up to touch her, but she stepped out of reach.

"You don't want to be in a relationship with someone who isn't into it," she said defensively. "You deserve better than that, Brett."

"Maybe you don't know what you want," he shot back.

"The rose. The stuffed animal. Showing up here unannounced, making a scene at my place of business. It's too much, Brett. Surely you can see that." She paused, because he was already shooting daggers at her with his glare.

"I already said that I didn't give you the whale. You didn't say anything about a rose before." This must've struck his macho core, based on his expression and how he puffed out his chest. "Someone's trying to win you over. I bet it's that jerk you were photographed with last night."

If he hadn't given her those gifts, then who had? Nash? An icy chill raced through her. *Win her over* weren't exactly the words she'd use to describe what Nash wanted from her. But Brett trying to force her to stay in a relationship she didn't want wasn't much better.

"It's not like that. Dade's an old friend," she defended. Brett had to be giving her those gifts. If not, someone was trying to mess with her…

And speak of the devil, Nash walked out of the

movie theater. He must've seen her, too, because he started making a beeline toward them. Tension caused her to tighten her grip on her cell phone. The thought of Nash and Brett being together was about as appealing as pouring gasoline onto a raging wildfire.

"I just bet he is." Brett moved within inches of her face with a glare that would've melted an iceberg. It wasn't going to work on her and he needed to be made aware of that fact. Back down from a bully and she might as well roll up the tent and leave town, because experience had taught her that once a bully knew he'd gotten to her, it was all over.

"I need to get back to work, Brett. The line is getting longer and my employees need my help." She could feel the heat of Nash's stare on her and prayed she could get away before those two clashed—cold air moving in on a heat wave. "Think about what I said and give me a little breathing room."

Brett's gaze locked on to Nash.

"Do you know him?" Too late for wishful thinking. This day seemed determined to get a whole lot worse.

"Not really." Carrie looked right in time to see Nash making progress toward her and Brett. She needed to think, to come up with something fast before those two massive storm systems collided. "I gotta go. If you can't understand my point of view, there isn't much else I can say anyway."

"We break up and you turn into some kind of sleaze?" The anger and disgust in Brett's voice sent fire shooting through her.

"How can you say something like that and wonder why I don't want to be with you anymore, Brett?" The words fired out, rapid and angry. It was one thing to cause a scene at her place of business, but to insult her to that degree caused a wildfire to rage inside her. She was barely keeping it together after last night anyway, and her nerves were about to snap.

Brett's hands fisted at his sides, and for a second she thought he might rear back and hit her. She backed up a couple of steps until her hands felt the tree. Out here, alone, she couldn't stop him from belting her. She felt around for something she could use as a weapon, just in case. There'd been a huge rock at the base of the tree. Maybe she could drop down and pick it up before he made a move.

Brett's gaze cut right and left sharply before fixating on something behind her.

She expected an argument, or more insults. Instead, Brett muttered something low under his breath before punching the tree. She ducked and her hand flew up to stop him, but he connected with the trunk anyway.

Gasps sounded from behind her and she assumed they came from her customers. *Great.* If she had to file a restraining order to keep him away, she would.

She'd do whatever it took to force him to keep his distance after this exchange.

Thankfully, he'd missed connecting with her face. She glanced at the line, flustered, and a part of her needed to stick up for herself for all those times she hadn't when she was little and being bullied by a foster sibling or parent.

"This isn't over, bitch," Brett shouted as he stalked off.

That last insult was fingernails on a chalkboard to Carrie.

"No, it isn't. You better stay away from me and my shop. Or I'll see to it that you do." She picked up the rock at her feet and tossed it at his back, regretting her actions the instant she released it.

The rock made contact. Brett spun around with a look on his face that sent an icy chill down her spine. Nash was closing in, and suddenly the air became thicker. Her chest squeezed. And then both men stopped, looking past her. A second later each turned tail in different directions and took off. Why was Nash still in town? Why was the carnival still sitting there packed up but not gone?

The minute she turned toward the sweet shop, she knew what had gotten into both men. *Dade.* He was stalking toward them. He was big—the military had filled him out—but it was the expression on his face that had to have been what had gotten to the men. Pure steel with a severe look that said *back off.*

Carrie's heart fluttered as she took a couple of steps in Dade's direction. She had no doubt that he could handle either Brett or Nash—or both at the same time, to be honest. His muscles rippled underneath his white T-shirt, and neither man would cause him to break a sweat. She appreciated the unfamiliar feeling of someone having her back for a change. For most of Carrie's life she'd been alone when bullies threatened, left to her own resources, and it was nice to have backup for once.

Don't get used to it, a little voice in the back of her head warned.

The roar of Brett's motorcycle engine cut angry lines through the now-stale afternoon air. He spun his back tire, spewing gravel at cars in the parking lot. A mother covered her child's eyes before stalking out of the line. A couple more followed. *Great.* All she could do was helplessly watch as her customers, her business, dissipated before her eyes.

"Looks like you've had one heck of a morning," Dade said, and when his gaze reached hers, a thousand butterflies released in her stomach. She had the sensation of falling with nothing to catch her and no care in the world.

That was not her life. Reality set in. Carrie had had to work for everything. Her life had been about struggle and stress. She'd believed that coming back to Cattle Barge and creating a successful business would make her feel something…like she belonged somewhere. This episode reminded her that there would always be someone there waiting to take away everything she'd worked for. That no matter how fast she ran toward the light, darkness would stalk her.

"I wouldn't argue that." She glanced at him and then focused on the line of customers that had dwindled, resigned to the fact that she'd never really belong anywhere. "I apologize for the disturbance. All of your treats are on the house today."

Creating a success out of her life meant more to her than anything, especially after the start she'd had in life. A very deep part of her needed to prove that she could be successful in her hometown. If she couldn't be happy in Cattle Barge—the one place she'd felt was home—she couldn't be happy anywhere.

"Have to say, this is the best ice cream I've ever had." Hearing Dade say that started to ease the tension causing the spot in her left shoulder to send stabbing pain radiating down her back.

She glanced from the line back to him, wishing she'd crawled under that rock instead of chunking it at Brett. "I better get to work. Thanks again for last night and today."

Carrie wanted to be seen as an equal in this community by everyone, especially Dade. Not someone who needed constant protection. The thought fired her up again.

An older woman whispered something about

the past repeating itself as she gave Carrie major side-eye before leaving the line.

And Carrie wondered if her past would always haunt her. If she'd always be that loveless orphan being passed around from home to home with no one to really love her.

"Who was that guy and what was he doing here?" Dade asked.

"He's my ex." Embarrassment heated her cheeks.

"Wish you'd hit him in the head with that rock instead of the back," Dade said with a smile that didn't reach his eyes. He pushed off the glass. "See you around."

Tears brimmed but there was no way she was going to let her customers see her break down. She turned away from Dade.

"Hey, Carrie," he said, and his voice was warmth pouring over her cold body.

She stopped. "Yeah."

"Be careful."

Chapter Six

A pounding noise shocked Carrie awake. Coco went berserk. Carrie shot to her feet and glanced around before shaking her head and struggling to get her bearings. The TV was on. She must've fallen asleep on the couch. Another five raps of fist on wood fired off behind her, shocking her fully awake.

She glanced down to make sure she was decent. Yoga pants and a T-shirt were respectable enough to answer the door. Right?

"It's okay, Coco," she soothed. This was no way to be jarred out of sleep. It felt like she was walking in slow motion, and she couldn't quite get her body to respond in the ways she wanted it to. She hoped everything was okay at the shop. Before her breakup with Brett, everything had been going well. *Too well*, a little voice reminded. Life had never been that smooth for Carrie for long. Memories of finally thinking she'd landed in the perfect foster home when, in fact, she'd moved into hell assaulted her.

The anger. The beatings. The suffocating feeling of being trapped with no means of escape.

Another round of rapid-fire knocks jarred her out of her reverie. She shoved the memory deep down and hurried to the door, tripping over a lump on the floor. She glanced down to see the orca shredded, white stuffing all over the carpet. Coco had gotten into the trash again. It was Carrie's fault for not taking it out before bed last night.

"Hold on. I'm coming." She stepped over the strewn pieces. Those needed to go to the outside trash. Coco had had a field day with the animal.

She wondered if Jerk Face neighbor had decided to stop by. Beating down her door to let her know that her trash had blown into his yard again seemed like something he'd do.

She glanced out the window as another round of banging practically split her head in two.

Sheriff Sawmill?

Carrie opened the door as her stomach sank. This couldn't possibly be good.

"What's going on, Sheriff?" she said as she opened the door and stepped aside to allow passage.

"Sorry to disturb you so late, ma'am." He tipped his hat with a look of apology. And exhaustion. The man looked beyond tired.

She glanced at the clock that read half past five a.m.

"Everything all right?" She held on to Coco's collar to keep the dog from jumping up on him.

He took two steps inside the door and stopped. "We need to talk and I'd like to do it in my office."

His words set off all kinds of warning bells. Her first thought was of her employees. "Did something happen to Eric or Harper?"

"No, ma'am."

"Did Nash do something?" She couldn't help but wonder if he'd harassed someone else.

"Not that I'm aware of," he responded.

"Is this about someone I know?" she asked, realizing the answer was pretty obvious.

He bowed his head. "I'm afraid so."

"If it's not my employees then who?"

"We'd be more comfortable having this conversation in my office." The sheriff's feet were in an athletic stance and his hands were clasped in front of him.

More warning sirens blared. Carrie noticed that Coco was trying to position herself in between her and the sheriff, growling.

"It's okay, girl." Carrie bent down to scratch Coco between the ears. "Whatever's going on I want to help. I just need a few minutes to let my dog out and get my purse."

Carrie coaxed Coco to the back door. She spun around to ask a question and almost walked into the sheriff.

"Sorry, ma'am. I have to keep you in my sight."

"What on earth do you mean by that? What's this about?"

"We'll have a chance to go over everything at my office."

"Do I need a lawyer?" Her mind started spinning with possibilities. She thought about the card Dade had given her with his cell number on it. He'd be up and already working.

"Not if you don't mind answering a few questions," he stated.

Carrie let her dog out while she stood in the door frame where Sheriff Sawmill could watch her. An uneasy feeling pounded her. Why would he need to keep her in sight?

"Sheriff, can I ask another question?"

"Yes, ma'am." There he went with that *ma'am* again. He was treating her formally, which gave her even more pause.

"Can I refuse to go with you?" She most likely knew the answer to the question before she asked, and yet she needed to hear him say the words anyway.

"I wouldn't advise it," Sheriff Sawmill said with a curious look.

"Do I get to know why you want to talk to me in your office before we leave my residence?" Her balled fist was on her hip, and her mind raced.

The sheriff bent his head down as though out of respect for something… What?

And then he released a breath and looked at her. "Brett Strawn was found dead in his home a few hours ago."

"Are you sure?" Air whooshed from her lungs and tears welled in her eyes. The sheriff must be mistaken. His information had to be wrong. "What happened?"

"That's what we're trying to figure out."

It was pitch-black on the way to the sheriff's office. Carrie's mind raced, unable to accept the news that someone she'd cared about was gone. Brett might not have been the man Carrie was in love with, and he'd been hard to deal with since the breakup, but she didn't wish him harm.

A swarm of media people circled the sheriff's vehicle as he parked in his reserved spot. She put her arm up to shield her face from the cameras as she wove her way through the crowd and inside the door.

Bright lights made it feel like daytime inside the building. Janis's desk was empty, as Carrie suspected it would be this time of morning. The wall clock read nearly six in the morning. The sun wouldn't be up for another hour or more.

A deputy met them in the hallway, and the sheriff turned to Carrie. "I'll let Deputy Kirkus take it from here."

Sawmill stepped aside to allow passage. She stood there, momentarily stunned, because the sheriff's office was to the right, but Kirkus was motioning for her to walk past it. She followed him down the hall toward a room at the end of the hallway, the farthest from an exit. Suddenly, she was glad that she'd thought of picking up Dade's business card and sliding it inside her purse before she left her house. She had a feeling that she was going to need a friend and a good lawyer.

A dark thought struck. Did the sheriff think she was somehow involved with Brett's death? The idea that she could have information was beyond anything she could imagine. Surely, this was protocol in an investigation and didn't mean what she feared.

Sheriff Sawmill might not be in the small rectangular room with them, but she would bet that he was listening. There wasn't room for much more than a table and a few chairs. Sawmill, no doubt, stood behind the two-way mirror on the long wall facing her. Any hope that she was being looked at as a witness died with the knowledge eyes watched her from the other side of that mirror. She was a suspect, as impossible as that sounded, and she wanted to scream that there was no way she would hurt anyone. Instinct told her to keep quiet instead.

"Where were you between the hours of midnight and 2:00 a.m.?" Deputy Kirkus asked, bringing any thought she'd had that this might be a misunderstanding crashing down around her.

"I was asleep on my couch." She watched his

gaze travel over her, assessing her. Her mind zipped through possibilities, as she was still trying to wrap her thoughts around the fact that Brett was gone. It couldn't be true, could it? She'd seen him earlier in the afternoon. Disbelief descended on her. There had to be an easy explanation for all this. Or there'd been a misunderstanding. "Are you sure it was him?"

The deputy nodded.

"So, you're positive that there's no chance there's been some mistake and he's okay?" She thought about the phone in her purse as she leaned back against the strap. She cupped her face in her hands. This couldn't be happening. Brett couldn't be…gone. Tears streamed, and she bit back a sob as reality slammed into her like hitting a tree at a hundred miles an hour.

"No, ma'am. I'm afraid not." Deputy Kirkus's voice was laced with respect in the way people spoke when they were talking about a deceased person, and that just splintered her heart even more.

"What happened to him? How was he killed?" He was young and healthy.

"We'll get to that in a minute," Kirkus said. "Were the two of you in a relationship?"

"Yes. Well. Not anymore, but we were." She didn't see what their status had to do with his death. She wanted to ask what Kirkus was doing in there with her when there was a killer on the loose, but instinct told her not to. The deputy had the same look of disbelief she'd seen when she'd told her case worker that the doughnut shop owner, Mr. Berger, had been trying to touch her in places that made her uncomfortable. The eyes always gave away how a person felt about what they were being told, and even a skilled investigator like Deputy Kirkus was no match for Carrie's experience at reading people. Being able to interpret the slightest shift in body language had helped her survive Mimi the drunk, a woman who could be nice until she opened a bottle of whiskey.

And that made dating Brett even more of a lapse in judgment. Even so, she didn't want to think badly of him after hearing the news that was rocking her world.

"When did the relationship end?" Kirkus continued.

"A couple of weeks ago. Two weeks and two days to be exact," she recalled.

"Who initiated it?" Kirkus's questions were invasive and awkward coming from a near stranger. Carrie didn't like the feeling of being interrogated even though she had nothing to hide.

"I did," she admitted. "Why?"

"How did he take the news you wanted to see other people?" Kirkus asked.

"That's not what I said," she defended.

Kirkus sat straighter in his chair. "What was the reason for the split?"

Carrie shrugged. "I wasn't having a good time with him anymore."

Kirkus barked a laugh.

"That's not what I mean. He became too possessive. We weren't right for each other." She glared at the unsympathetic deputy.

"You believe he left a flower on your car the other night," Kirkus continued.

"Yes. But what does that have to do—"

"A part of you wanted him out of the way."

"He showed up at my business ranting and making a scene. He grabbed my arm so hard…" She showed him the bruises.

"Mr. Strawn was an inconvenience to you, wasn't he?"

"What are you accusing me of?" Carrie pushed to standing.

"I'm just looking for the truth." Kirkus folded his arms and leaned back in his chair.

"Will you please tell me what happened to Brett?" Carrie couldn't bring herself to say the other words—words like *killed* and *murdered*. "I can't help if you don't give me anything to go on."

"Mr. Strawn was electrocuted." A physical shiver rocked Deputy Kirkus.

Her mind snapped to a job site, but how on earth would that happen between the hours of—what had he said?—midnight and 2:00 a.m.? "I guess I don't understand. You said he was at home?"

She was still trying to absorb the information.

"Yes, ma'am," Kirkus said with a small head shake.

Shock shot through her. A picture was starting to emerge. Brett had been electrocuted in his own home.

"How do you know he was…that *it* happened on purpose?" Where was Tyson, his pit bull?

"I don't know too many people who would toss a hair dryer into the shower while they're still in it." His words were heavy and too straightforward. She figured some of that was from lack of sleep, given the dark cradles underneath his dull gray eyes. For someone in his midforties, Kirkus's hair was a little too gray for his age, his physical demeanor a little too fatigued-looking.

"Wait. It happened in his bathroom?" Now her mind really was racing. Again, her thoughts jumped to some kind of freak accident.

"When was the last time you had contact with Mr. Strawn?" Kirkus leaned forward and rested his elbows on the table. He motioned for her to sit so she did.

"Yesterday morning. There were witnesses. He showed up to my shop angry and threatened me," she said.

"You didn't call him or text?"

"I didn't. And I didn't answer any of his attempts to reach me, either. It's why he said he came to the shop in the first place." She stared at Kirkus. Did he believe her? "Feel free to pull my cell phone records and check."

"We will." Kirkus softened his approach a little when he said, "This is a murder investigation, ma'am. I'm not trying to offend you. What can you tell me about Mr. Strawn's other relationships? Was he seeing anyone else?"

"Not that I know of," she said.

"What about fights? Had he been in an argument with anybody other than you lately?"

"I'd been avoiding him, so I couldn't tell you." She crossed her legs and rocked her foot back and forth.

"Did he owe money to anyone?" Kirkus's gaze intensified on her.

"Brett owed money to a contractor." She snapped her fingers. "His name was Jimmy something. Oh, what was his last name? I remember him saying something about that before we broke up. He'd seemed unsettled and a little scared, which I distinctly remember because he usually put on a tough guy routine in front of me."

Carrie glanced at the deputy. He sat there, shoulders forward and clasped hands resting on the table.

"Maybe you should write this down," she urged.

He pulled a small recording device from his shirt pocket and set it down in front of her. "Please, continue."

She flashed her eyes at him. "Brett owed Jimmy-what's-his-name money."

"And Jimmy is what kind of contractor?" the deputy asked.

"He does tile," she said.

"Is there anyone you can think of who might want him out of the picture or benefit if he was gone?" Kirkus asked, still studying her.

"I stayed out of his work affairs and we really hadn't dated long enough for me to know everything about him." She scanned her memory. "That being said I can't think of anyone off the top of my head."

"Mr. Strawn had a dog." The door opened behind her and the deputy nodded toward whoever stood in the doorway.

"Of course he did. Tyson." It had taken Carrie weeks before she would go to Brett's house after he'd explained that he'd trained the dog to protect his equipment on job sites. Once she got to know Tyson, she loved him and got on Brett for being too hard on him when he did something Brett didn't like. In fact, his cruel side had been one of the many reasons she'd decided to walk away from the relationship in the first place. "Oh, no. What happened? Is Tyson okay?"

"The dog's fine." The sheriff walked in and stood beside her. "In fact, he was so calm that he let the killer walk right past him to get to the bathroom where the victim was showering."

Carrie sat there, dumbfounded, for a long moment. Reality crashed down around her like a carefully constructed building tumbling down in an earthquake. The handwriting on the wall said she'd been rousted awake in the middle of the night because she was the primary suspect.

Anger burst through her. Cooperating so they could find Brett's killer was one thing. Being accused of *being* Brett's killer was another story altogether.

"Am I under arrest, Sheriff?" she asked.

"No, ma'am."

"Suspicion?" she pressed.

"How well did you know that dog?" The sheriff took out a Zantac packet and opened it. He popped a pill in his mouth and dry swallowed.

"I'd been to Brett's house dozens of times. I knew Tyson." The sheriff might not realize it, but this interview was about to be over.

"Well enough to walk right past him when his master was home?" The sheriff returned the half-empty packet to his pocket.

"Yes." Carrie reached inside her purse.

"I'll be back in minute." The sheriff walked out the door, leaving it open and giving her the feeling that she was no longer a trapped animal. She was, though. The deputy followed Sawmill into the hallway, where the two men spoke in hushed tones.

While she waited for the sheriff to return, she located Dade's card and pressed it flat to her palm. With her cell phone in the other hand, she started to punch in the number, unsure of what she'd say except that maybe she needed his help and a recommendation for a good attorney.

"I'd hold off on making that call if I were you." Deputy Kirkus's voice startled her.

She gasped. "Why?"

"We're just having a conversation," Deputy Kirkus said, but his tone had changed.

"I'd like to make a phone call. Is there a law against it?" she asked, turning to face him so she could get a good read on his body language. She didn't like the accusation in his tone, but looking at him only made it worse. His frame blanketed the door. He was tall and thick around the midsection. Too much sitting in a cruiser, she thought.

"No, ma'am." There he went with that *ma'am* business again.

"Well, if I'm not doing anything wrong, I'd like a little privacy, if you don't mind," she said, needing to see if he would leave her alone.

"Is there anyone who can verify where you've been tonight?" Deputy Kirkus asked.

Carrie blew out a breath. "I'd like to make that phone call now."

"Are you sure you want to do this?" Kirkus's brow arched, and the worry lines bracketing his mouth intensified.

"Make a call? Yes." Carrie tightened her grip on the card, rubbing her thumb along the embossed letters.

The deputy leaned against the doorjamb and folded his arms. "Forgive me for bringing up the past, but you were moved around in the system quite a bit as a child, weren't you?"

Where'd that come from? "I'm not sure what my childhood has to do with my life today and especially with Brett."

"It's just that you ended up with the Berger family, if memory serves," he continued. He needed to get to the point.

Carrie crossed her legs and rocked her foot back and forth. "I still don't see—" It dawned on her where he was going with this. "I can assure you that I'm perfectly stable."

"It's not healthy for a kid to get passed around so much, is it?" he continued, and fire lit in her chest.

"What are you trying to say, Deputy Kirkus?" She locked on to his gaze. "That I'm unstable? That I'm crazy because I didn't have the best childhood? I'm not the only one who ever had problems while growing up."

"I've seen the photos," he said, and he was getting a little too close for comfort.

"And?"

"Mr. Strawn had a reputation for putting his hands on women." He bowed his head, and she couldn't really tell if he was being respectful of the dead or sorry for the accusation sitting in the air between them.

"If I understand this correctly, you're accusing me of getting rid of him because he hurt me," she clarified.

"Abuse does things to people, especially kids. Maybe you'd had enough and this guy caused you to make a mistake," he stated.

"The only thing I'm fed up with is being accused of something I didn't do." She stood and shouldered her purse.

Kirkus's hands went up in the surrender position. "Hold on there. No one's accusing you of anything."

"Except having a bad childhood, right?" She tapped her toe against the tile as anger built inside her. It didn't matter what she said or did. She'd never break free from people judging her, not here or anywhere else. "I'm upset now. Are you afraid I'm going to do something stupid?"

He shook his head.

"So it seems that I can be angry and still behave like a normal person." She took a deep breath meant to calm herself. "The reason Brett and I broke up is because I saw a side to him that I didn't like. In case you're wondering, he never put a hand on me."

"The dots aren't hard to connect," Kirkus countered with an apologetic look. "A jury might feel the same way."

The thought of living the nightmares of her past all over again, and especially for public consumption, caused her to shiver. "I doubt a jury would convict anyone who'd been at home with her dog while someone she once cared about was murdered."

"Says you," he stated. "You say that you were home with your dog. Unfortunately, your pet can't corroborate your story."

"Whatever happened to being innocent until proven guilty?" she countered, reminding herself to breathe. The walls felt like they were closing in around her and she needed to get outside for some fresh air.

"Like I said, I'm just thinking like a jury," he claimed.

A noise tore from Carrie's throat. "Let's hope juries have more common sense than that, Deputy."

"I'll get the sheriff." He turned toward the hall but didn't leave the door frame.

Carrie started to pace.

"Ma'am, I'm afraid I have to ask you to sit down." There was nothing friendly about his expression or posture now.

Carrie prayed the card in her hand would give her strength. "Why's that, Deputy? Am I not free to go anymore?"

"It's in your best interest to cooperate," he stated with a frown.

"I asked this before and I'm asking it again. Am I under arrest?" All he'd told her so far was that her ex-boyfriend had been electrocuted—the thought still ripped her heart out—and the person responsible had walked right past his dog to do it. She wasn't the only person in the world who knew Tyson, and Brett would have a long line of people he'd upset at one time or another. The guy didn't always use tact when trying to get a point across.

"No, ma'am. And I'd like to keep it that way." He leaned against the doorjamb again.

"So would I. And since I haven't done anything wrong, I don't expect any change in that statement." She stalked toward him. "So if you'll excuse me, I just learned that someone I once cared about is dead. I'd like to go home and cry before taking a shower and finding someone to open my shop this morning, because I have a feeling this is going to be one heck of an awful day."

The deputy didn't move.

"Excuse me," she said, looking him square in the eye. His were a dull, watery gray outlined by red. Too many late nights. Too much coffee. Too much sitting.

His judgment was horribly off, and she'd blame those three things for him standing there, blocking the door, and not the fact that he really might think she'd killed Brett.

Chapter Seven

"Deputy, I'd like to go home," Carrie stated boldly, realizing that she didn't have any leverage in this situation. She didn't even have a ride. It didn't matter. The walls were closing in, and she could scarcely believe the accusation hanging in the air. Asking to walk through the door would tell her exactly where she stood. *At least for the moment*, a little voice reminded her, because even if they allowed her to leave, that didn't mean it was over. Brett would still be *gone*—she fought against the onslaught of emotion threatening to crack her in two—and she could be hauled back in at any time.

"The sheriff picked you up?" Kirkus craned his neck, looking behind him before acknowledging Carrie's request and stepping aside.

"Yes," she conceded.

"If you can be patient a few more minutes, someone will give you—"

Carrie's hand was already up and waving off the

deputy. It was far too late for talking, and she had no plans to stick around the sheriff's office a minute longer than she absolutely had to. She recognized the stall tactic for what it was. "I can manage on my own."

She stalked past Kirkus without a sideways glance. She'd walk home if she had to. Dade would be up but possibly out of cell range and she wanted to get out of there now. There had to be an app for a car service. She hadn't needed one until now and didn't have the first clue what to do to find the app. The App Store? Could she call for a car this early? She had no idea how it worked, but that wouldn't stop her.

If not an app, then what? Or who? One of her employees would pick her up in a heartbeat, but how would she explain being in the sheriff's office following Brett's murder?

A little voice in the back of her mind said, *Dade*. She rubbed her thumb against the embossed letters one more time. She hated the thought of disturbing him. But hold on. Living on the ranch, wouldn't he already be awake and working?

She stalked outside into the balmy air. More rain threatened, another rarity for August in Texas, but shocking truths were lining up tonight. Media people descended on her. She turned tail toward the lobby as tears threatened to overwhelm her. She made a beeline for the women's restroom and cleared the door before the first sob tore from her throat.

A stall opened, and an overwrought Ms. Strawn stepped out. Her eyes were puffy and red as she zeroed in on Carrie.

"What did you do to my boy?" Ms. Strawn came at her with balled fists.

"I would never hurt him," Carrie defended herself, and a flash of guilt assaulted her because she already had just not in the same way.

Carrie caught the woman's arms as she thrust them toward her. The older woman was surprisingly strong for someone in her late fifties who was on disability. Carrie guessed it was grief causing her to act out, to wrongly accuse. She couldn't possibly believe that Carrie would hurt another human being. Could she?

"I'm so sorry about what happened," Carrie offered, releasing the woman's hands.

Brett's mother exhaled, her tall, willowy frame shrinking like air out of a balloon.

Ms. Strawn drew back to smack Carrie, who sidestepped the flat palm coming toward her.

"You ought to be in jail for what you did to my boy," Ms. Strawn seethed. "I knew you'd cause something like this. Bad stuff clings to you and hurts everyone around except you."

Carrie backed against the sink and gripped the porcelain. Words could be so much more damaging than physical blows.

Ms. Strawn stepped forward, pointing her index

finger at Carrie's face. "Mark my words. You won't get away with this."

"I didn't do anything." Why was she defending herself to a woman who didn't care about finding out the truth?

"I know all about you and what you said happened. I told my son to steer clear of you from the get-go. You're a liar and a murderer," Ms. Strawn accused. "And now my boy is paying the ultimate price."

"I wouldn't hurt Brett." Carrie stepped out of reach of the shaky finger being pointed at her.

"You did. And now my boy's…" Ms. Strawn shrank back, unable to finish. She covered her mouth with her hand, and tears streamed down her sallow cheeks.

The door opened and Brett's sister, Brenda, caught sight of what was going on. She darted to her mother's side.

"Let's go, Mama," Brenda said, shooting a nasty look at Carrie. "She's already done enough. Leave it alone and let the sheriff do his job."

The woman collapsed against her sturdy daughter.

"She'll pay for what she's done," Ms. Strawn cried out.

"I know she will," Brenda soothed, glancing back to shoot another dagger at Carrie with her eyes.

Carrie stood there, stunned and motionless for a few minutes. It took several more before her hands stopped shaking enough to make the call to Dade. She could only pray he was in cell phone range. He picked up on the second ring.

At the sound of his voice, a sob burst through. She could barely gather her thoughts before blurting out, "I'm so sorry to bother you but I didn't know who else to call and so much has happened I don't even know where to start."

"Slow down, Carrie. Where are you?" His warm rumble of a voice washed over her, bringing a sense of calm that she knew better than to allow. It wouldn't last. Good things never did in her life.

"I'm at the sheriff's office," she stated as calmly as she could manage before another sob retched from her throat.

"What happened?" By the tone of his voice, it occurred to her that he thought Nash had pulled another stunt. It was reassuring that his first thought was she was hurt or in danger rather than her being a suspect in a murder investigation.

"It's Brett," she said, unable to speak the horrible truth without tears streaming down her cheeks. "Something's happened. He's...*gone*."

"I'll be right there," he said. The line was dead before she could say another word.

Just thinking about it made her stomach churn and threaten to revolt. She moved to the sink and splashed water on her face before locating a rubber band in her handbag and pulling her hair back into a ponytail and off her face.

Brett was gone. The two of them had been in a bad argument. And now she was a suspect in his murder.

It seemed the fear that had haunted her entire life was real.

The storm cloud that had followed Carrie had returned, and it might just swallow her whole this time.

"DADE," CARRIE SAID the moment he walked through the doors of the police station. She charged toward him and buried her face in his chest as he wrapped his arms around her.

He could see that she'd been crying even though she tried to cover it. He could feel her trembling in his arms even though she tried to appear brave. And he could sense her fear even though her chin rose in defiance as she met his gaze.

"The sheriff just showed up at my house and brought me here for questioning," she stated, so much torment in her voice. "They think I'm involved in Brett's murder."

"That's crazy," he defended as shock and anger fired through him. This was not the best time to have a sit-down with the sheriff about how off base the man was, but Dade had no plans to gloss over this. Sawmill couldn't possibly believe Carrie was guilty of murdering her ex-boyfriend. And if he did, Dade had something to say to the man to straighten him out. He and Sawmill hadn't said a bad word between them, but that was about to change if he didn't leave Carrie alone.

"I didn't have anyone else to call," she said.

"You did the right thing," he reassured, thinking that he needed to get her the hell out of there. More anger fired through his veins at the thought she'd be questioned for her ex's murder under the circumstances. Dade might not've been in touch with Carrie for a long time, but he still knew her well enough to know she was one of the kindest people. She didn't deserve to be treated like this, especially with her background. She'd been through hell and back, and he hadn't been there to protect her.

Where did that come from?

He'd analyze that later. Right now, the problem he faced was getting her out of the sheriff's office without drawing more unwanted media attention.

Dade tucked her under his arm. The forecast called for rain, and it was starting to sprinkle outside. That got him thinking as he walked into the temporary command post that had been set up to take leads on his father's murder. "Does anyone have an umbrella?"

A volunteer motioned toward a coatrack while recording details from a phone call.

"I'd owe you one if you'd let me borrow this." Dade picked up a small red offering and held it up.

The volunteer was on a call, but she glanced up

anyway. Her gaze fixed on Carrie for a split second before connecting with Dade's. She covered the receiver and said, "Go ahead and use it. I'll make do."

Dade mouthed a thank-you before fishing a wad of cash out of his pocket. He peeled off a few twenties and set them on the table in front of the older woman. Her eyes brightened and she smiled before quickly returning to the call in progress.

"Let's take you home," he said to Carrie as he opened the umbrella before exiting through the front door. He could hide her face from the media attention for now. But they'd been seen together the other night, and that probably wasn't good for Carrie. Being seen with him could have the media digging into her painful past.

After depositing her on the passenger side of his truck, Dade took the driver's seat. "I'm sorry about all those reporters."

"Thank you for picking me up," she said, and he hated how small and vulnerable she sounded. This was not the Carrie he was used to, but he understood why she'd be coming from that place and his protective instincts flared.

"We'll figure this out. We have Ed, who will arrange a defense for you should this go to court. He's the best and he'll make sure the truth comes to light," he said, liking the fact that he was thinking up a game plan to help her with a murder defense even less. "Let's get him on the phone right now."

Dade used hands-free Bluetooth technology to call the family lawyer.

Ed picked up on the first ring. "What's going on?"

The lawyer skipped perfunctory greetings. No one would call him at this hour with good news.

"I have Carrie Palmer in the truck with me. You're on speaker," Dade supplied.

"Okay. What's going on with Miss Palmer?" He sounded surprisingly awake now. The family lawyer's ability to snap to strategic thinking on little to no sleep had always amazed Dade.

"Her ex, Brett—" He glanced at Carrie.

"Strawn," she supplied with an overwhelmed quality to her voice.

"Brett Strawn was murdered earlier this evening," Dade finished.

"Okay," Ed said, and Dade could almost hear the dots connecting while he offered sincere-sounding condolences.

"How long ago did the relationship end?" Ed asked.

"It's been a couple of weeks," she said after thanking him.

"Forgive the question, but was the breakup amicable?" His voice was a study in calm.

"Not really," she admitted.

"When investigators dig into this case, and I'm assuming the sheriff already picked you up for questioning, what kinds of communications between the two of you will they find?" he asked.

"What do you mean? Like emails? Texts?" She sounded disoriented and a little confused. No doubt still in shock.

"Exactly like that," he encouraged.

"Mostly texts and unreturned phone calls," she said.

"I take it you were the one who ended the relationship," Ed stated.

"Yes."

"Did he ask for another chance?"

"Almost constantly." This time she sounded deflated and guilty. Both understandable emotions, given the circumstances.

"And this caused discord between you," Ed concluded.

"Yes. It did. A great deal, actually." More of that defeated tone came across.

"Were you considering taking him back?" Ed probed.

Dade didn't want to acknowledge how eager he was to hear the answer to that question. Certainly not to her and especially not to himself.

"Not one bit," she said with assuredness.

"I know this is going to sound harsh given the situation, but had he become a nuisance?" Ed was forging ahead.

"Yes. He came to my business to try to convince

me to take him back and didn't like it when I said I needed time to think," she admitted.

"How'd that go?" Ed's voice raised an octave.

Dade remembered the fight she and her ex had had in the parking lot and the crowd of people who'd witnessed the exchange. At the time, he'd been proud of Carrie for standing up for herself, but he would've handled the situation differently if he'd known this was where it would end up.

"About as badly as it could've. He shouted, which frightened my customers. A few left. He yelled at me." She stopped.

"Did he try to lay a hand on you?" Ed asked, his tone even.

"Yes. We exchanged heated words in the parking lot, and he reared his hand back to strike me. I backed up against a tree, saw a rock and chucked it at him as he walked away," she admitted. "I was angry, but I would never..."

A couple of beats passed before anyone spoke again.

"Did the sheriff give you any idea of what happened to Mr. Strawn?" Ed asked.

"He was electrocuted in the shower," she said, again with the same small voice.

Ed apologized again.

Carrie released a sob, and her hand came up to cover her mouth.

"Why do you think the sheriff came to her first?"

Dade asked, realizing she needed a minute before she'd be able to continue. Her emotions were understandably raw.

"It's routine. I'm sure someone witnessed their fight, and it's customary in a murder investigation to look to those closest to the victim." Ed paused. "In this case, it sounds like the sheriff brought her in so he could get a feel for her emotions. See if she had a good alibi and he could rule her out."

"I was at home, alone with my dog," she supplied.

"Can anyone corroborate your story?" Ed asked.

"No." Carrie went dead silent.

Carrie exhaled, sounding like she was barely keeping hold of her emotions.

"What's the next move?" Dade asked.

"Just stay low until I speak to the sheriff to see what evidence he might have that could put Carrie at the scene," he said.

"His mother was there. I ran into her in the bathroom. She accused me…" Carrie's voice trailed off as though remembering the exchange was too hard. Or hurtful.

"I take it she doesn't like you." Ed's sympathy was a welcome reprieve.

"Not a bit," Carrie supplied.

"Is there anything else the sheriff mentioned that I should know?" Ed asked after a thoughtful pause.

"He mentioned something about Tyson." Carrie sat a little straighter in the seat. "Tyson is Brett's dog.

The killer walked right past him and dropped a hair dryer in the shower."

"So, the assumption they're making is that the victim knew his killer." Ed's tone shifted. "That makes even more sense why the sheriff wanted to talk to you first."

"Tyson would never let a stranger walk into the house without a fight. He'd been trained to guard construction sites and Brett didn't let a lot of people around his dog," she supplied.

"Did Mr. Strawn bring a lot of people to his home?" Ed asked.

"He kept a lot of tools there. So, no. He didn't trust people not to steal and that's why he got Tyson in the first place. To guard his equipment." Carrie glanced at Dade, and that one look sent electric currents rocketing through him. He chalked them up to his need to protect her on overdrive.

"Was his business going well?" Ed perked up at the last piece of information.

"He always seemed to have plenty of work, but he supported his mother and sister, so that didn't leave him as much to live on. The neighborhood where he lives is a little sketchy. He also recruited workers from around the neighborhood when he needed more hands." She wiped away tears before giving the family lawyer a few names of Brett's associates, saying she'd given the same ones to the deputy earlier.

"Any chance you were present during the fight, Dade?" Ed's tone changed.

"Yes."

Chapter Eight

"I'm sorry," Dade said to Carrie after ending the call with Ed.

"We fought in front of everyone yesterday. That has to be why they'd think I did something like this to someone I once cared about." She twisted her hands together in her lap. The lost look had returned.

Those words, this situation were abrupt warnings to keep his distance. His last girlfriend had been tangled up in a messy situation with her ex, and Dade had sworn off any involvement with another woman in the same predicament. If he and Carrie hadn't been so close at one time, he would have connected her with Ed or a great defense lawyer and then walked away.

Experience had taught him these situations were messy. In the case of his ex, Naomi, she'd never been able to get over the loss of her high school sweetheart, who had died on the football practice field senior year. When her relationship with Dade be-

came serious enough for him to consider a trip to
the jeweler, she'd sprang it on him that she could
never truly love anyone other than her ex. The only
problem was that she'd kept Dade in the dark and
the relationship going until he caught her with another guy. She'd blamed her overwrought emotions
for the affair. Dade had licked a few wounds over the
whole ordeal at the time. Now, he was mostly glad
he'd dodged that bullet and hadn't married someone
who couldn't let go of the past.

"Who can you call to open the shop today?" He
needed to remember how it felt to have his heart
trampled on and keep his distance, especially as he
was trying to get a handle on his emotions following the Mav's death.

"Once news gets out that the sheriff thinks I'm a
murderer, no one's going to bring their kids into my
shop for ice cream." There was a defeated quality
to her tone.

He hoped the town of Cattle Barge was more sup-
portive than that and yet he'd witnessed the people
giving her dirty looks and leaving her business because her ex was causing a scene. She was probably
right. Once details of her past emerged—something
she'd never spoken about to him and he'd never felt
right digging into on his own—then all the history-
repeating-itself accusations would fly. Dade needed
to think of a way to spare her now, because he'd let
her down before and he couldn't live with himself

if he did it twice. Her friendship was worth more than that to him.

"Everything'll be fine. You'll see." The words were hollow no matter how much he wanted them to be true.

Her lack of response said she knew it, too.

"I'd like to stay with you for a while." He pulled up in front of her house and cut off the engine.

"Are you sure? I know you need to get back to the ranch." Carrie opened the passenger door. Her voice was even, and he couldn't read her.

"Dalton can cover for me," he reassured her.

At the door, Carrie's hands shook as she tried to position the key properly, clueing him into her emotions. He covered her hand with his and she stiffened like she was preparing for something before she handed him the key. She didn't immediately move away from his touch, and he could see that she needed comfort—the kind of comfort he knew better than to give while she was this vulnerable. He unlocked the door, opened it for her and hesitated before following her inside.

Damn slippery slope he was about to walk onto. His life was already in chaos and hers had been turned upside down. Neither one of them was in a position to think clearly. The attraction that had been sizzling between them was a distraction they couldn't afford.

Dade flexed and released his fingers. They still

vibrated with tension from touching her. It was so far beyond a bad idea to go inside her home that Dade almost thought better of it. Almost. Because before he could overanalyze the situation, the sweetest little dog came barreling past his legs.

"Coco," Carrie shouted a little too late. The critter had already bolted outside and off the porch. A frustrated Carrie called for her dog.

Dade put two fingers to his lips, slicked his tongue across them and whistled.

The little firecracker immediately cut right twice and was on her way back toward the door at full speed. Carrie stepped aside in time for the excited pup to fly inside. Dade stepped in after the dog and closed the door behind him.

Carrie looked at him, stunned. "How on earth did you do that?"

He smiled. "It was nothing."

"That's the first time she's ever..." Her eyes started welling up again.

"It's because I'm not familiar. She most likely came back to protect you," he said.

"That usually means hackles raised and rapid-fire barks," Carrie argued.

The dog returned to Dade, alternating between sniffing his boots and barking up at him excitedly. Her entire backside wagged like crazy. He bent down and scratched her behind the ears. "See, it's the foreign smells."

"I doubt it." Carrie looked down at her with a frown.

"Being brought up on a ranch helps when it comes to animals," Dade said by way of explanation.

Carrie stared down at her dog for a long moment. "Guess so."

"I'll put on a pot of coffee." She bit back a yawn. It was easy to tell that she was trying to cover her exhaustion with a half-hearted smile. It was a lot like trying to put a Band-Aid on a geyser.

"I can do that if you point me to the kitchen," he offered.

"Great. It's over there." She motioned left. "I'll let Coco out the back. If she'll still come to me."

Carrie called her dog as she walked toward the door. Coco followed Dade into the kitchen.

"What did you do? Rub fresh meat on your boots?" Carrie stood there, hands out, exacerbated.

"Coco and I are going to get to know each other in the kitchen while you find someone to cover at the sweet shop." Dade leaned against the counter and folded his arms. "No arguments."

"How about another plan? I'll freshen up and then we'll see where I stand," she countered.

"As I remember from playing tag on the playground, you were always good at getting your way. Even when you were tagged out, you'd figure out a way to negotiate your way back into the game."

"Then you know there's no point fighting me on

this," she said with a smile that was a lot more genuine this time. The dimple on her left cheek emerged, and an overwhelming urge to kiss it shot through Dade. He needed to keep his hormones in check. Yes, Carrie was a beautiful woman, and in the midst of all their problems—and combined they were doozies—he wanted nothing less than to get lost in her, with her. But since that idea was about as smart as sweetening his coffee with cyanide, he forced himself to focus on something productive—making coffee.

While he could hear water running in the bathroom down the hall, he texted Dalton.

You've been gone a lot lately, everything okay? Dalton texted back.

Need a change of pace, Dade responded.

That all?

Dade thought for a long, hard minute, and then texted, A break from the ranch, too.

You need anything? came Dalton's response.

Not me. Helping a friend.

You need an assist? Dalton responded.

How many times had they used that term on the playground as kids during a basketball game? Their relationship was one of the few good things that had carried over from childhood. The two of them were solid through thick and thin.

Thanks for not asking who it is.

Figure you'll say when you're ready, Dalton responded.

A thought struck. Was he dodging his own problems in order to help Carrie? He wouldn't deny how much easier it was to focus on someone else's rather than face his own. Besides, his couldn't be fixed. The Mav was gone. There was no going back and erasing the harsh words Dade had said to him. He'd regretted them instantly. Before he could find the right words to apologize, there'd been that fishing pole, the note, and then the Mav had been killed. All those unspoken words left to sour and fester.

His cell buzzed in his hand, jerking his thoughts to the present.

Take the time you need, bro.

Dade reassured his brother that he intended to pull his weight around the ranch and would explain everything later. He didn't want to talk about Carrie or analyze his deep-seated need to protect her.

Pictures of the two of them were most likely on every local news outlet by now and his family would be able to put two and two together as to whom he'd been helping. Ella already knew, but she'd keep his confidence. Everyone else would be aware soon enough if they weren't already. No matter how much everyone tried to avoid the news lately, it seemed unavoidable. Dalton wouldn't ask unnecessary questions. Ella might, but only because she was concerned about keeping everyone safe. Dade would have to address the situation with his family and let them know what was going on soon. Not today, though.

When he really thought about the way the sheriff was investigating his father's murder in contrast to Carrie's situation, he was surprised Sawmill hadn't hauled him in for questioning. He and Dalton had suffered plenty of abuse over the years at the hands of the Mav. They both lived at the ranch and had had complicated relationships with the man. Wouldn't that make them suspects?

Why had Sawmill jumped to Carrie so quickly? Considering he'd brought her in for questioning in the early morning hours, the sheriff couldn't have had a chance to talk to witnesses, could he? Unless he had someone who'd walked in and placed Carrie at the murder scene. Dade made a few mental notes of questions he had for Ed after the lawyer spoke to the sheriff.

Dade had taken the first sip of black coffee by the time Carrie reemerged. He tried not to focus on how thin the material of her T-shirt was as her full breasts lifted with every breath she took.

Coco was happily curled up next to his boots as he poured a cup for Carrie.

"Thank you." She took the offering, and he ignored the frisson of heat where their fingers grazed. "I reached Harper. She'll open the shop for me."

The heat between them would only get him in more trouble, and his emotions were already getting away from him. Carrie offered a peek of light and that made her even more dangerous, which was why he needed to resist the urge to reach out and her and pull her in his arms, taking in her fresh-from-the-shower flowery scent.

And he could do that even though his fingers flexed, acting as if with a mind of their own.

He could control this attraction that was trying to get away from him, like he'd handled every tough situation he faced, with focus and determination.

Or so he tried to convince himself.

CARRIE TOOK A sip of the freshly brewed coffee and then set the cup on the counter. Seeing the insides ripped out of the once-stuffed whale sitting on top of the dryer almost kicked off a fresh wave of tears. Brett had denied being the one to give it to her, but he was the only reasonable option. No one else knew her well enough to know orcas were her favorites.

After letting Coco go outside, Carrie pointed to

the stuffed animal. "I'd like to get that thing out of here."

"You didn't mention this before." Dade picked up the orca and examined it.

"My first thought after Brett was Nash, but it can't be him, can it? I mean, he's gone. The festival packed up and left already, didn't it?" she asked.

Dade pulled out his smartphone and opened the internet application. He entered AquaPlay Festival. "They're in Nacogdoches, opening tonight."

"That's not far." Her face paled. "But at least he's not here."

"Ed has a meeting set up in a couple of hours to probe the sheriff and find out what law enforcement is doing to find the person responsible for Brett's death." He realized he was getting his fingerprints all over potential evidence. He set the stuffed animal down and took a step back.

"What's wrong?" Carrie had always been perceptive.

"Other than destroying any chance they could get DNA from the orca?" Damn. He blew out a frustrated breath. And then another when he saw the look of horror on her face.

"I didn't even think about that." She muttered the same curse he was thinking and it was a lot stronger than *damn*. "After Coco chewing on it and me handling it, the only things they'll find are dog DNA and teeth marks."

"I don't know how easy it would've been to pull prints off fabric anyway. I'll let Ed know what's going on here. He'll be able to tell us what to do." Dade fired off a text. He didn't like the feeling of being helpless. "Is there something significant about this being a whale? Does it mean something important to you?"

She'd never told a soul the reason, just that she loved them.

A hot tear stung as it rolled down her cheek.

"When I was little, maybe seven or eight—" she shrugged "—I can't remember exactly how old I was, only that I lived with this sweet old woman. She was the kind of grandmother everyone wished they had. Her name was Mildred and her husband's name was Bronson. They were the kindest people I think I've ever met, aside from you and your brother and sisters."

Dade seemed taken back by the comparison. "Us? Kind? Nah. We could be better people."

She doubted it. His oldest sister worked tirelessly to make Cattle Barge a better place to live for everyone. She was involved in more charities than Carrie could count and had been targeted for murder because of her work in trying to build an additional animal shelter. Dade and Dalton were probably two of the best men she'd ever met. *And especially Dade*, a little voice pointed out.

"Bronson retired and wanted to spend their last

few years together traveling the world. Mildred—
Grandma Millie to us—refused, because she wanted
to see her foster work through. They'd taken in me
and another girl, Sandy, who was a teenager. Then
Bronson got some bad health news. I don't remember
what happened exactly. But he got sick, and Grandma
Millie almost wore herself out taking care of him.
We pitched in as much as we could, but now I realize how much of a burden we must've been to her."

"She sounds like an amazing woman," Dade said,
and his words were a blanket of comfort around her.

"I know he was taking a lot of medicine for a
while. He was bedridden. And then he got up and
walked out the back door. He sat in the backyard for
an hour. Every day after, he improved until he got
close to where his health was before." A surprising
spring of tears leaked from her eyes. She wiped them
away with an apology.

"Don't be sorry for crying."

"She hugged us and told us how much she loved
us but that she'd almost lost her Bronson. She wanted
to spend as much time as she could with him. We all
crumbled onto the floor in a puddle of tears. I'm not
sure that I even knew what I was crying about. I just
didn't like seeing her sad. I had no understanding of
how much my life was about to change or that she
meant we weren't going to be part of the picture anymore." Carrie paused to wipe away a few stray tears.

"I'm sure that was a hard decision for her to

make." Dade's gaze pierced her. There was so much compassion embedded deep behind the fortress he'd constructed.

"Before she allowed our case workers to take us, she wanted to spend one last weekend together. Looking back, they didn't have much money, so it must've cost a fortune for them to take us to the whale park in San Antonio. They'd bought a small RV, and we stayed in a nearby park. I just remember how hot it was outside, and then suddenly I didn't care because I was watching this massive animal do all these amazing tricks. It was the most awe-inspiring thing I'd ever seen."

"She sounds like an amazing woman," Dade offered with such sincerity Carrie nearly released all the pent-up emotion bottled up inside her.

The couple didn't have much and had planned to travel the country on a shoestring budget. Losing Grandma Millie had left a hole in Carrie's heart that threated to swallow her. The next group home wasn't so kind, and the others…

Carrie didn't want to go there, so she gripped the stuffed animal and walked outside to the trash. Her neighbor's king-cab truck was gone, and she wondered where he went. He'd disappear for days on end, sometimes weeks. She opened the lid to the plastic container and dropped the orca inside. More unexpected tears sprang from her eyes, but she immediately wiped them away.

Dade stood in her kitchen, sipping his coffee. Emotions roared through Carrie. Instead of analyzing them, she walked straight toward Dade, pushed up on her tiptoes and kissed him. He stiffened for a split second before wrapping his arms around her waist. She threaded her fingers through his hair, and he deepened the kiss.

His big frame corded again, and she almost thought she'd done something she was about to regret. And then his hands, rough but gentle, cupped her cheeks and he tilted her face to gain better access to her mouth. His full lips covered hers, and she leaned into his hard body. He was strong and brave and everything she wasn't at the moment. His kiss was so tender, and yet so hungry, it robbed her of breath.

She brought her hands up to his muscled chest and flattened her palms against him. She smoothed her fingers over the ridges of his pecs as he pressed his lips harder against hers. Her breath hitched when she looked up at him and saw so much hunger there, hunger that matched her own.

Dade seemed to come to his senses first, pulling back just enough that if he spoke his lips would still brush against hers. She could feel his breath on her and taste him, a mix of peppermint and coffee.

He'd done the right thing. The kiss was supposed to slap her back to reality, stop her from overthinking. But the heat that had been missing in every other kiss for her entire life had her mind churning even more.

And the attraction that she knew better than to allow took deeper root.

DADE HAD WANTED to kiss Carrie from the moment he'd seen her again in the alley behind her shop. After hearing more about what had happened to her years ago…all he wanted to do was protect her. She'd lost so many people. Others had abused her. He'd tried to avoid listening to talk about the neglect she'd suffered after becoming a ward of the state. She'd needed him when she'd returned to Cattle Barge. He could see it in her eyes, even if she couldn't admit it to him or herself. And what had he done?

He'd been a typical teenager too caught up in his own issues to do what he should've done then…step up and protect her.

Since then, his mind always circled back to that one time with her before she'd disappeared. They'd been in seventh grade, and he'd asked if she wanted to study together. He'd taken her to a popular hangout spot, the Barn. The two of them had been laughing and talking easily, and he'd liked the way he felt around her.

Until his friends had shown up. One of his jock buddies, Todd, had stopped by.

"What are you doing here with her? Shaylee tried

to call your house earlier and invite you out with us tonight," Todd had said.

"Nothing," Dade had said defensively. Then he'd motioned toward the stack of unopened books on the table. "Trying to make sure I pass Harris's English class."

Todd had made some arrogant crack that Dade had laughed at before walking away.

Dade would never forget the look in Carrie's eyes.

"I gotta go. Study. So I can pass and get out, away from the jerks in this town," she'd said, pushing past him. Now he realized she'd been too strong to cry in front of him.

She'd gotten away from him so fast that by the time he discerned just how much of a jerk he'd been and figured out a way to apologize, she was long gone. She'd been in such a hurry that she'd forgotten her books on the table. He'd tried to return them but she refused to see him after that day, so he'd stopped trying. He'd let her down in the worst way and still felt residual guilt because it wasn't long after that a relative had claimed her. Then, she'd been abandoned and transferred to another home…*the* other home with the Bergers.

She'd disappeared not long after. And he'd never had a chance to explain what he was struggling to understand for himself as a teen—his feelings.

He'd never experienced that kind of intensity with anyone before. He'd been too young and dumb to know what to do with it. His lack of maturity had caused him to handle the whole situation wrong, and before he could make things right she'd been shuffled around again. She returned the summer before senior year and she'd grown into those long limbs. In fact, she was even more beautiful than she'd been before, and everyone seemed to notice, except her.

Dade wasn't making excuses for himself. Everyone thought life as a Butler was easy because his family had money. He had just as many hardships as the next guy. The Mav had worried all his money would make his sons soft. He'd come down hard on Dade and his brother, saying he was making men out of them.

Dade, in turn, had signed up for the military the day he could enlist. Basic might've been hard for some, but not Dade. In more ways than one, it had been his salvation. He'd let go of the anger—or so he'd thought, until the Mav had tried to make amends. But he never really trusted anyone again except his brother and sisters. He'd constructed walls that made it difficult for anything or anyone to penetrate. The Butler kids had been forced to band together to survive their childhood with Maverick Mike.

Dade knew one thing was certain. Thinking about the past never made it better, and it sure as hell didn't change anything. Dade judged people by their present actions. He looked at Carrie, who was studying him curiously. Intelligent, beautiful Carrie.

"Say something," she said, and he could tell that, for once, she was having trouble reading him.

He stood there, looking into her beautiful eyes. He fisted his hands to keep himself from reaching out to touch her silky skin.

And then a little voice in the back of his head reminded him how much he'd regret not doing just that. Touching her. Kissing her. *Oh, hell.*

Throwing common sense out the window, he stalked toward her, took her in his arms and kissed her again.

She responded, tunneling her fingers into his hair and moving her sweet lips against his. All arguments imploded, and the world righted itself for just that one moment when she was in his arms.

This time she pulled away first. Dade sure as hell couldn't have done it.

She blinked up at him, and he couldn't read her. "Your job in the military train you to run toward danger?"

"Yes. What does that have to do with you?"

"I'll hurt you, Dade. I won't mean to, but I will." She stepped away and turned her back to him.

Whatever craziness was going on in her life didn't matter this time. "You need to know that I have no plans to walk away from you until I've seen this through."

She rubbed her arms as though a chill had run up them, but it was hot outside.

"Will you let me?" he asked.

There was no hesitation when she nodded.

He spun her around, hauled her against his chest and kissed her again.

And there was so much power in that one kiss he knew he had to figure out a way to help her without touching her again.

Chapter Nine

Carrie woke after a couple hours of sleep. Glancing at the clock beside her bed, she realized it was almost one o'clock in the afternoon. Panic gripped her that she'd somehow forgotten to open the store and then she remembered making the call to Harper earlier. Images of everything she'd worked so hard to build tumbling down the drain smacked her in the face. It was a sobering thought and one she didn't want to give much energy to.

Her movement woke Coco, who was curled up at the foot of the bed. She hopped down and Carrie immediately missed her warmth.

There was a note propped up on the nightstand from Dade. She picked up the folded paper and turned the edges over with her fingers, thinking about the couple of kisses they'd shared before they'd come to their senses and put a little distance between them. He'd insisted on staying to make sure she was okay.

"Call when you wake up," the note read. She didn't make calls before coffee if she could avoid it.

Thoughts of last night at the sheriff's office and of Brett's murder stalked her, sitting like a heavy lump in her chest that made breathing almost impossible. At least Nash was gone.

She pushed up on her arms, still in disbelief any of this could be happening.

Maybe coffee could somehow wake her up from the nightmare of learning that someone she once cared about was gone. *Brett.* Her heart felt like it might burst out of her chest. He was so young, and she couldn't even imagine how much pain he'd felt in those final few moments of his life.

Carrie threw her legs over the side of the bed and walked into the adjacent bathroom to splash cold water on her face and brush her teeth.

Her ringtone belted out from down the hall as she rinsed. Her heart stuttered, because her immediate thought had been that it was most likely Brett calling. But he wouldn't be contacting her ever again. Carrie's legs went rubbery, and she had to grip the wall with both hands to steady herself.

Don't look up. Don't look down. Keep forging ahead and life will catch up. Mrs. Sanders's words wound through Carrie's thoughts. She must've just turned sixteen years old when she'd lived in her group home. The kind woman had been diagnosed with a rare bone cancer and had had to shut down her operation.

Carrie's heart lurched. The short time she'd lived with Mrs. Sanders had given her a chance to begin the healing process after that last brutal attack. The thought that Mrs. Sanders might be watching over Brett now offered some small measure of relief. Mrs. Sanders had a way of bringing hope to the hopeless. Brett might've turned out to be a jerk but Carrie didn't wish him dead.

Fighting against the onslaught of emotion building, threatening, Carrie got to her phone as the call rolled to voice mail. She didn't recognize the number, which was probably just as well. She wasn't in the mood to speak to anyone anyway. Although based on the number of messages on her phone, quite a few people were trying to reach her. All from numbers she didn't recognize as she thumbed through the log.

There were dozens of unread messages from Brett, waiting. His last attempt to reach her had been less than an hour before his death. She still couldn't grasp the thought that Brett was gone. Even though she knew it was true on some level, her mind wanted to argue against the fact. Somehow offer proof that this was all some kind of awful dream and she'd wake any minute to find that he was very much alive.

She glanced at the spot on the counter where the stuffed orca had been, grateful it was gone. A text from Dade said that Ed had stopped by this morning with a deputy to pick it up even though there might not be any evidence on it. Dade had shown them where it was outside in the trash.

Coco stood at the back door, whimpering.

"Okay, sweet girl. I'll let you out." Coffee could wait another minute. And then she'd call Dade. Carrie unlocked and opened the back door.

Coco hopped out but then spun around. Something on the ground had caught her attention. Carrie gasped, and her pulse skyrocketed. Hold on. It was probably nothing more than a cricket. She leaned forward and looked down, catching a glimpse of red. A single rose.

Carrie's heart pounded painfully against her ribs. She shooed Coco away from the wilted flower and bent over to pick it up. Then she remembered the fingerprints and froze. Could Brett have left it? No, that was impossible.

Someone was messing with her. Anger ripped through her, and her skin flamed.

Coco bolted toward her, causing Carrie to jump. She was on edge and needed to calm down. No, what she needed was a gallon of caffeine so she could think more clearly. She stared at the flower like it might come to life and attack her. There was no way she was picking it up.

After her dog darted inside, she locked the door and stalked over to her phone. A mix of anger and frustration and helplessness—which made her even angrier—fueled her steps. The minute she gripped her cell, it rang. She jumped, dropped it and took a step back. Okay, now she was letting every little thing get to her.

Glancing at the screen as she picked it up, she saw that the call was coming from an unknown source. Anger pulsed through her as she answered. Whoever was on the other end was about to get an earful. Before she could speak, a male voice cut her off.

"Ms. Palmer?" the masculine voice asked. She didn't recognize it.

"Yes." Impatience rolled off her in waves.

"My name is Darion Jones and I'm with *News-Now!* on the cable channel—"

She ended the call before he could finish. How had the media gotten hold of her private cell phone number?

News of Brett's murder had to be out by now. She would think that the sheriff would want to keep an ongoing investigation as quiet as possible. Her employees would never give out her personal information to a stranger, especially not with everything going on. The only person who was capable of doing such a thing was Brett's mother—he'd given his mother her number for emergencies, if she couldn't reach Brett first.

Carrie needed to have a conversation with Dade's lawyer. Speaking of whom, she needed to call Dade. But a conversation before caffeine was a bad idea, and she also needed to figure out what to do with that rose.

The first sip of coffee couldn't make a dent in how exhausted she felt. She put a few ice cubes in a glass. They crackled as she poured the brown liquid over them. Iced coffee was quicker, and she drained the glass a minute later before pouring a second cup, warm this time. She had a feeling that she'd need all the extra energy she could get today.

Equipped with a little more of her mental faculties, she called Dade. He answered on the first ring.

"Everything okay?" was his first question.

"What time did you leave my house?" She intentionally dodged his question. Things couldn't be less okay.

"Around nine o'clock," he said. "Why?"

"You didn't happen to see anything suspicious at the back door, did you?" She got straight to the point. She and Dade had always been able to talk to each other. Well, up until things had changed between them in high school.

"No. I let Coco out before I left and there wasn't anything at the back door. Why? What did you find?" His concern was outlined in his rich, dark voice—a voice that wrapped around her and promised everything would be okay. But everything would not be all right. A man was dead. She was suspected of murder. And someone had decided this would be a good time to mess with her. Nash? Or someone else? Was there someone from her past who had come back to torment her?

"What is it, Carrie?" There was so much concern in his tone. His voice was the calm in a raging storm, but she knew better than to allow the comfort. Nothing was okay. Nothing would be right again. This was Carrie's life, history repeating itself. Any time she found something good to hold on to, it would slip out of her grip.

"What if it was his mom? Or sister? Maybe he told them about it." She gasped, thinking out loud.

"Tell me what you're talking about, Carrie. What did you find on your doorstep?" His strong male voice demanded an answer.

"The rose." The words coming out of her mouth sounded impossible even to her when she heard them spoken aloud.

"You didn't touch it, did you?" he asked.

"No. But Coco started clawing at it," she informed.

"Stay where you are. I'm on my way."

"Okay." The two exchanged goodbyes.

Carrie double-checked the back door, making sure it was locked before pacing in the kitchen. She needed something to do, something to occupy her thoughts. She glanced into the laundry room and remembered the load of laundry that needed to be put away. First, she checked in with work. Her mind was too scattered to go over numbers or the details of orders but she got a high-level update from Harper.

Her employee mentioned that reporters were showing up, asking questions.

A few minutes later, a few deep breaths, and her nerves were beginning to settle with the busywork. All she had to do was wait until Dade got there, she thought as she pulled out the last item from the laundry basket, a pair of jogging shorts.

But hold on a minute. Where was the sundress she'd worn a few days ago? She might be going crazy—and that was a very real possibility lately— but she could've sworn she'd washed it with her jogging shorts.

She got up and bolted toward the closet to check. Not there. How about the clothes hamper? Her next stop was the master bathroom. The hamper had clothes from the last two days in it and nothing else.

Carrie wasn't going crazy. The dress was missing.

DADE HADN'T MADE it halfway to Carrie's house when his cell ringtone cut through the air. He answered it hands-free.

"Someone's been in my house," she said breathlessly, and he could hear the panic in her voice.

"When? Now?" A shot of panic gripped him. He wasn't close enough to get to her if an intruder was in the house.

"No. The other day," she supplied, and the tightness in his chest loosened up a notch. He was far from comfortable, but at least there was no immediate threat. But someone had been there this morning if they'd left the flower. He would've seen it when he let Coco out otherwise.

"How do you know?" Dade needed to be certain she wasn't in danger. And he sure as hell would handle things differently moving forward. The first of which would be to add security to her residence.

"One of my dresses is missing. My favorite jogging suit disappeared, too, but I thought Brett had it and now I'm not so sure." She paused a beat. "Oh, no. There were crumbs on the floor the other day. Dog treats that Coco used to love, but I stopped buying them because the vet said she was putting on weight too fast. I thought she found a leftover bag, but I was sure I'd tossed them all out."

"Stay right where you are. I'll call Ed."

"I don't want to be here and I have to go into the sweet shop. My employees need to see that I'm okay. And—" Carrie was a little breathless.

"Slow down. Tell me what you need me to do."

"There's nothing you can do, Dade. You can't fix this. Not with Brett's murderer still on the loose and some unknown person messing with me. My world is suddenly spinning out of control."

"We'll find out who killed Brett and we'll put a stop to whoever is bothering you," he reassured her, but she was dangerously close to a complete meltdown.

"I keep thinking about that *thing* on my back

porch and I don't want to be inside my house right now. Bad luck is like a boomerang and keeps coming back." Based on her quick bursts of air in between words he figured she was pacing.

"I'll see to it the deputy takes it in as evidence. I can assure you it won't return." He'd ask if there was any way he was going to convince her to stay put, but he didn't much care for investing time in lost causes. Especially when he already knew the answer. She was as stubborn as she was beautiful.

"I'll take Coco to work with me. She has a bed in my office from the early days before I could afford employees and I literally spent every waking moment at work." She was offering assurances to him that she'd be okay. Her mind was already made up, and there was precious little he could do to change it.

Carrie having her dog with her at all times did make him feel a little more comfortable. Still, he'd been on edge since hearing about Brett's murder. Since another rose had showed up, he worried about something else, too—her safety while at home. "I'll meet you at the shop."

Dade ended the call and banked a U-turn at the first intersection. The sweet shop was actually closer than her house, so he beat her there and parked in the empty lot across the street. He needed to make a couple of calls while he made sure she arrived intact. And then he'd take care of her house.

There was chaos across the street at her sweet

shop. Slipping past the clump of media crews to get inside without drawing more unwanted attention would be next to impossible. At least the festival workers were gone. That should bring Carrie a small sense of relief that she wouldn't have to deal with Nash on top of everything else. Which also, most likely, meant that he wasn't responsible for the flower. Her ex was instantly ruled out, but someone connected to him, like his mother, was a real possibility. Especially after the outburst at the sheriff's office that had upset Carrie.

Dade cut off the engine and grabbed his cell. His first contact was Ed.

"I just got out of a meeting with the sheriff," Ed started right in.

"Where does Carrie stand?" Her status as a witness or suspect heavily influenced their next couple of moves.

"He's looking at her as a witness, but that could change," Staples supplied. "Samuel Jenkins corroborated the story about Nash from the other night. It's giving her more credibility."

"I also think I can help out with that." He told Ed about the flower and the missing clothes.

"The sheriff needs to know immediately." Ed said he'd call Dade back after updating Sawmill. It didn't take more than a couple of minutes for Dade's cell to ring and the two of them to pick up the conversation where they'd left off.

"What did Sawmill think?" Dade asked.

"He found it interesting and assured me that he'll do everything he can to find the responsible party," Ed said. "We need to take measures to ensure her safety while the investigation continues."

"You think the person leaving her gifts and Brett's murderer are the one and the same?" Dade was already on that trail.

"It's suspicious. I hope I impressed the sheriff with that thinking," Ed supplied.

Now that there was a murder involved, her case should rise on Sawmill's priority list. "Did he say what evidence he has that she could possibly be involved in Brett's murder?"

"Right now, he has a statement from the deceased's mother indicating that Carrie had threatened her son if he didn't leave her alone," Ed said. "There are others who have come forward to witness the argument from yesterday and the fact that she attacked him with a rock."

Dade released a disgusted grunt.

"I know what you're going to say, and I also know that's not what happened. I'm telling you what people think they saw." Ed's sympathy came through the line. At least Ed didn't believe the lies. His confidence in Carrie would go a long way toward building a strong defense. There was nothing like truth and righteous belief to make a man go to the ends of the earth to find proof of innocence.

"Even if Carrie threatened her ex, and I doubt that she did, I don't believe Brett would've taken them seriously. Not with the way I witnessed the man treat her in front of her shop. The guy was trying to bully her back into a relationship with him." Dade white-knuckled the steering wheel with his free hand. *Unbelievable.*

"The sheriff requested a statement from you."

"I figured that was coming." Dade was more than happy to provide his side of the story, especially if it could help Carrie.

"Witnesses put you at the scene of their falling-out, and some believe that the two of you are in a relationship." Ed's voice changed and Dade immediately sensed the reason.

"I didn't hurt the man, no matter how much I dislike the kind of men who think it's fine and dandy to put a hand on a woman. I'd be willing to take a lie detector test if that'll clear my name and keep the sheriff from chasing down crazy theories." Dade knew all about how lost the sheriff's office could get during an investigation—they weren't any closer to finding out who'd murdered the Mav.

"That shouldn't be necessary, and I didn't suspect you in the least. I need to ask Carrie if she'll relinquish phone records to the sheriff," Ed said.

"She has nothing to hide, so I doubt that'll be a problem." Dade was confident on that point.

"I didn't think so."

"Can't the sheriff subpoena her records, though?" Dade figured either way the sheriff would get what he wanted.

"This would be a lot faster, and her cooperation will go a long way toward keeping her where we want her, which is on the witness list. Plus, if she volunteers the information, the sheriff will see her as aiding his investigation. It'll win points."

"She'll be here in a few minutes. Tell me what you need her to do." Dade didn't figure there'd be any pushback from Carrie. She wanted Brett's murder solved.

Dade listened as Ed rattled off a couple of items to add to today's to-do list. At the top was giving the sheriff access to her cell phone records and her house. Dade took notes before asking, "Did the sheriff mention anything about the complaint she filed the other night against the guy who threatened her in the alley?"

"He mentioned a festival worker known as Nash, who his office is tracking down," Ed said.

How hard could it be to find a man who worked with a festival that publicized its schedule? "I can probably tell him where to look with a quick online search."

"You might find the festival, but you won't find him. He can't be located," Ed stated.

"I saw him yesterday late morning in the parking lot of Carrie's shop," Dade supplied.

"Then that makes you the last person to see him." There was dread in Ed's voice.

"What about the people who witnessed the argument yesterday? Surely they saw him, too." Dade didn't like the sound of those words.

"They weren't looking for him, so even if they saw him they most likely wouldn't remember." Ed had a point.

"What you're telling me is the man could be anywhere." Dade raked his hand through his hair, trying to tame the curls. Nash might've left that flower at her doorstep after all.

"According to his employer, he's most likely sleeping off a hangover on someone's couch. Or at least that was the excuse he gave when he didn't show up for work last month for three consecutive days," Ed supplied.

"If he has a drinking problem, why would they hire him to work around kids?" Dade asked.

"Apparently he's in recovery, but he seems to be having trouble keeping it together since losing his brother," Ed said. "His boss told him three strikes and he's out. This is the third."

"Which means he won't be showing up at work asking for another chance," Dade said.

"I asked the same question. His employer says he'll be back. Said he has no other family and the news about his brother hit him hard. His boss said he's a decent person when he's sober," Ed supplied.

Dade wasn't so sure about that. But then, Carrie

had said the man had had alcohol on his breath when he'd threatened her. Dade released the white-knuckle grip he had on the steering wheel. "What happened to his brother?"

"Overdose," Ed supplied. "He'd been an addict for most of his life."

"I'm sorry."

Dade maintained a moment of silence.

"There's no history of crimes against women with Nash," Ed supplied.

With this investigation, Dade hated the thought that rumors would abound, possibly dredging up painful memories for her.

"Is there anything in Carrie's past I need to know about?" Ed asked.

"She had it tough growing up, being tossed around from foster family to group home," Dade shared. "There was abuse, in some cases severe."

"I'm sorry to hear that." Ed paused for a couple of beats. "I'm even sorrier that I have to ask if she's been involved in illegal activity."

"You wouldn't be good at your job if you weren't thorough," he conceded. His protective instincts always flared when it came to Carrie. Speaking of whom, he saw her car slow down and then pass right by the parking lot. "I don't know everything she's endured, but she has amazing internal strength to have gotten where she is today after the start in life she had."

Dade's phone buzzed in his hand, indicating another call was coming through.

"It's Carrie. I'll have to call you back," he said to Ed.

"Let me know when the sheriff can access her house and make sure no one goes inside until evidence is collected," Ed reminded him before ending the call.

"Where are you?" Carrie asked as soon as Dade answered.

"I'm in the lot across the street from your shop." He caught sight of a trio making a beeline straight toward him—reporters? They might've recognized his truck. "But I'm about to be on the move. Can your business at the shop wait until later?"

A long sigh came through the line. "Doesn't seem like I have much of a choice."

"Meet me at Grover's," he said.

"The auto repair shop on Beekman Avenue?" she asked.

"That's the one. And Carrie—" he started.

"What is it, Dade?"

He didn't want to tell her, but she needed to know. "Nash hasn't reported to work—"

She gasped.

"No one knows where he is, so be on the lookout in case you get to Grover's before I do."

Chapter Ten

Carrie drove slowly to Grover's, scanning the area at every stoplight, looking for Nash. The thought of him being out there, somewhere, didn't do good things to her pulse, and for a split second she questioned whether he could have something to do with Brett's murder.

Logic said it was impossible because Nash had no idea who Brett was other than seeing her talk to him in the parking lot yesterday. Unless there was a connection she didn't know about.

Nash had been far more intimidated by Dade and so would most likely try to erase him in order to get to Carrie. Right? But nothing made sense anymore and she couldn't rule anything out.

After being brought up to date on Dade's conversation with Ed, Carrie surmised that Nash was a transient festival worker who was losing his battle with alcoholism. He had no history of rape or assault, although Carrie feared he might've been well on his way to his first that night in the alley. And, there was no way Tyson knew who Nash was. *Tyson.* What would happen to him now that Brett was gone? He was too aggressive with other dogs for her to feel safe leaving him alone with Coco, or Carrie would volunteer to take him in herself. But then, Ms. Strawn would surely want her son's dog.

She circled the block until she saw Dade's truck pull into the parking lot, not wanting to take any chances of being alone even though she had her dog. Based on Coco's performance with the neighbor and seeing how easily she'd warmed up to Dade—although Carrie couldn't fault her dog there—she didn't want to tempt fate. She parked next to him and locked her doors. Coco eagerly followed Carrie into Dade's truck.

"We'll keep a low profile until the buzz settles down at your shop," he said. "With all the media surrounding the case, I filled my family in on the way over. They'd like to offer help in any way they can. I've arranged for extra security to control who has access to your property and keep an eye on your home. Media might blitz the place as soon as someone figures out your house is being treated like a crime scene."

"Right. I hadn't even thought of reporters." She appreciated Dade's thoughtfulness even more. Emotions tugged at Carrie's heart, emotions like acceptance and warmth. Experience had taught her they'd be ripped away before she could get used to them.

She buckled into her seat and thanked him with as much sincerity as she could without breaking the emotional dam protecting her heart.

"Ed thinks it would be best if you turned your phone over to the sheriff." She was trying to absorb everything. Dade was covering a lot of bases for her, and life was moving at such a high rate of speed that she needed to kick into high gear to keep up.

"Okay." She paused to process what he was saying.

"Sawmill wants my statement, too, so we should swing by together. I doubt it'll take long," he said. "Ed informed me that Samuel went in for questioning and basically said the same things we did about Nash the other night, which bought us some credibility."

"I keep going over and over everything in my head, and I can't figure out who could've gotten past Tyson," she finally said, taking a sip of the coffee Dade had offered. Carrie absently stroked Coco, who was curled up on the front seat between her and Dade.

"A dog bred and trained to protect is usually good at his job," Dade agreed.

Carrie searched her brain for the missing piece, the link that would click everything together and paint the picture. "None of this makes sense."

"I know." His voice was calm and held none of the

panic hers did. She wanted to get lost in that feeling, if only for an hour or two.

"It just keeps following me," she said quietly.

"What does?" Dade kept his gaze on the stretch of road in front of them. He was so good at moving forward despite everything going on around him.

"A dark cloud."

"There's no such thing." His reaction was so fast, so instinctual that she almost believed him.

"I'll lose my business. Everything I've worked for." She hated the defeat in her voice, but it hurt to say those words.

"It won't come to that." Easy for Dade to say. Everything in Carrie's life had been fleeting. This would be no different. And there was no way a man like Dade could understand where she was coming from. The Butler kids had always been close. It was common knowledge that if one was in trouble, the others rallied around to help, no questions asked. Carrie had no idea what it would feel like to have so many people around ready to catch her if she fell. The concept was foreign to someone used to being alone and looking out for herself. And it wasn't self-pity causing these thoughts. It was truth. And her strength had always been in looking at what she had to deal with honestly and then figuring out a way to survive.

Dade must've sensed her thinking because he added, "I won't let your business fail because of this."

His words were so quiet she almost didn't hear them. There was a promise there that even Dade couldn't deliver on. He couldn't take away the darkness that followed her. Not even Dade Butler could bring Brett back to life, stop the person who was messing with her or keep her business afloat.

A FEW QUIET days could hardly erase the shock of Brett's murder. National broadcasts had picked up Brett's story, reporting on a wave of crime in small-town Texas, and his mother and sister had already given several tearful interviews, some of which Carrie was certain they'd received payment for. At least Ed had warned them about going on air and accusing Carrie of murder. He'd been quick to point out that he'd file a lawsuit if that was the case.

Ms. Strawn had lost her only son and Carrie could only imagine how horrible that must be for any mother, especially one who depended on him for pretty much everything. She could forgive his mother for her outburst and the interviews. Carrie refocused on stirring the ice cream, grateful that she was at work and had something to distract her. She had had to close the front of the shop because of reporters and curiosity seekers, but there were enough standing out-of-town delivery orders to keep her head above water. At least that part of her business was still going strong. How long would it take for news to spread and other businesses to distance themselves from her?

The media camped out every day but seemed to have no idea that she was coming in during the middle of the night to work, and she wanted to keep it that way. Any time her mind drifted to what people must think of she wanted to give up. Why was it so important that the people of Cattle Barge accepted her?

Because she loved this town, a little voice reminded her. Because this was the only place that had ever felt like home, the voice continued. And, the voice repeated, if she couldn't fit in here, then where?

Hand mixing the ice cream, having something to focus on besides all the craziness going on around her, was keeping her sane. The trick was to stir the mixture every three hours for thirty minutes as it froze.

Carrie had slept very little her first six months of business before she could afford to hire help. Having a successful business had made her feel proud of herself for the first time. She couldn't let that be taken from her, even though all she really wanted to do was crawl into bed and stay there. Having security control access to her home brought a sense of relief on one front. On another it made her feel like she was in prison.

Coco had been quiet for the last twenty minutes, and Carrie had left the door to her office open so she could hear her dog in case she needed something. An animal wasn't allowed in the food prep area due to health regulations. She had a bed in the office and another spot out front where she liked to curl up when the store was closed.

Carrie's new throwaway phone buzzed as she put the last of the ice cream away. She'd given her old phone to the sheriff for analysis and, even though she was innocent of doing anything wrong, it didn't feel that way. Giving up her phone also brought a strange sense of relief. Was it all those unreturned messages from Brett that had had her on edge and feeling guilty? Dade was calling exactly when he said he would, at quarter to four in the morning.

"How'd it go tonight?" he asked.

"Better. I think I have everything under control again, but I need to be back early tomorrow night to keep things rolling," she replied, not wanting to admit how much hearing his voice calmed the raging winds stalking her.

"Ever think about taking a night off?" he asked.

She almost blurted out, *To do what?* She hadn't had much of a social life since moving to Cattle Barge. Brett had been her "get back on the horse" attempt, and look how that had turned out. Besides, she didn't want to be seen in public. She could only imagine the rumors swirling around town about her. She had to have round-the-clock security at home to keep everyone at bay. "I might not have a choice if I can't open my shop any time soon."

"I'm out back," he said.

She thanked him and ended the call, coaxing Coco out of bed and toward the back door. On second thought, she doubled back to make sure the front was locked, too. Recent events had her unwilling to take any chances.

The door was locked, so she put Coco on her leash and headed out. Her gaze immediately flew to the twin headlights peering at her from the alley. Her eyes hurt looking at them, which Dade must've realized, because he immediately turned them off.

Carrie saw stars. She blinked a few times before throwing her shoulder into the door and locking it.

With no front-end sales, she would be on shaky ground very soon. She hoped everything would blow over and get back to normal before the business she loved, that she'd built from nothing, completely tanked. The shop was all she had. Admitting that made her life seem truly empty as a sense of defeat overwhelmed her.

Don't go there. Don't think like that. Everything will be fine.

But fine wasn't a given in Carrie's life. And darkness stalked her like cancer cells waiting for the right trigger. She glanced at the alley with a prickly feeling running down her spine. It was the sensation of being watched.

Anger roared through her as she fisted her hand tighter around Coco's leash. Because the feeling was just a feeling. There was no one out there watching her. And that feeling didn't get to win today. It was probably just her frustration clouding her emotions, but the revelation felt good.

"Did you speak to Ed today?" she asked Dade as Coco settled into her comfortable spot between them.

"There's nothing new to report," Dade supplied. He'd given his statement days ago, and a deputy had collected evidence from her house.

"I'm guessing that Nash still hasn't turned up yet." There'd been no sign of him in Cattle Barge as far as she could tell. If he had been the one to…cause harm to Brett…wouldn't he be smart enough to get out of town?

Dade shook his head.

"What about the stuffed animal or the rose? Did they find any prints on either?" Carrie was getting short on patience as the sheriff worked through the details of her case at what felt like a snail's pace.

"Forensics is still working on it. That, or the sheriff's office isn't releasing the information to us." He navigated onto the main road, his headlights leading the way.

"Or anyone else. It'd be all over the news if they had." Carrie had been avoiding coverage as much as she could. She'd bought a temporary phone at a convenience store that couldn't be traced. News of the complaint she'd filed against Nash got out, and it seemed everyone in town was looking for him.

There was even more reason for him to hide now. And the sheriff might never find him, considering they already knew that he didn't have a cell phone—which was unimaginable to her in this day and age—and he seemed to have gone off the grid completely.

Dade kept her posted when the occasional friend of Nash's made news by giving an exclusive interview talking about how close the two had been and how this or that person had tried to help Nash battle his demons. The trail from him leaving the festival had gone cold almost immediately. It seemed that no one knew where he was and he could keep on hiding indefinitely. At least her cell phone records along with witnesses had cast suspicion about Brett's murder away from her.

"Ed mentioned that Nash's employer had said the reason his foreman had decided to stay around Cattle Barge was to give them time to find him before they headed onto the next city," Dade said.

"And then they eventually had to leave in order to be in Nacogdoches?" she asked.

Dade nodded.

"I keep thinking that Nash has something to do with all this, Dade. I do. But he couldn't have known about the stuffed whale." She paused a beat. "What are the chances that Nash even knew Brett?"

"There's no way to be sure," Dade said.

"What if Nash decided to stick around and asked Brett for work?" Her mind was spinning with possibilities.

"He could've been looking to settle down somewhere," Dade agreed.

"Brett had a temper. It wouldn't have taken much to set him off, and especially if Nash was crazy enough to mention something about me," she continued, feeling a little momentum gathering. "He said something in the alley about thinking about sticking around town. At the time, I just thought he was saying whatever came to his mind. I was so disgusted by him that all I could focus on was getting away. But now, what if?"

What if.

"Think Brett would've invited him over to his house?" Dade asked.

"Anything's possible, I guess." She shrugged because that's where she hit a wall. "Tyson wouldn't have let him by that night after only one meeting. He would've stopped him. Tyson was trained to go after anything suspicious, and the neighbors didn't report any barking."

"A stranger, even if Tyson had met him once before, would never get past him without a fight," Dade said. "And if that's the case, there would've been evidence of a struggle. Ed said the person opened up the front door and would've walked right past the dog."

"We're right back where we started." She released a heavy sigh.

Dade pulled up next to her house and parked before following her inside.

"Not exactly. Nash could still be around," he said. "We didn't consider that possibility."

The thought scared her more than anything else, but he had a point.

"He could've met people and decided to stick around to party," Dade said. "There are a few hotspots around the area for people so inclined."

"The old Hiller land." She'd never gone to it when she was in high school, but she'd heard there was always alcohol flowing. The property sat between two ranches, and neither family laid claim to it. It was mostly pasture with a few trees. She'd heard of bonfires and parties. "You used to go there with… what was her name? Shaylee?"

Dade didn't seem thrilled that she'd brought up a girl he'd dated. She started to apologize but couldn't figure why she'd be doing so. Surely he wasn't embarrassed by having gone out with one of the most popular girls at their school, if not *the* most popular.

His jaw muscle ticked, and it looked like it was taking great restraint not to say the first thing that came to his mind.

Coco barked at the back door, interrupting the moment of tense silence.

Chapter Eleven

"You ever think about having a security system installed in your home?" Dade needed to change the subject. He didn't like talking about his past with Carrie, especially not after the way he'd treated her back then. He couldn't go back and change things that had happened. Moving forward, he could help her out with more security. Whatever Coco had barked at was gone by the time they checked.

"I called the other day when everything started getting…weird, for lack of a better term. Every company I talked to said they were backed up. I couldn't get an appointment until next month." It made sense that everyone would be in a panic after the crime wave in Cattle Barge.

"That's not good enough." Dade called Terrell Landry, head of security at the ranch, and made arrangements. He turned to Carrie after ending the call. "Someone will be here tomorrow evening to install a system."

"What's it like to be able to snap your fingers and get anything you want?" There was a hint of admiration in her tone, but Dade didn't like the implication. Because she was saying that being a Butler made his life a walk in the park compared to everyone else's, and the truth couldn't be further. Her comment shouldn't grate on him like it did.

"I'm trying to help, if you hadn't noticed," he countered with a little more ire than he'd planned.

Her hands came up. "I'm sorry. I didn't mean to offend you. I've just fought tooth and nail my whole life for what I have, and it's all about to disappear. Everything comes so easy for you."

"You think it's easy being the son of Maverick Mike Butler?" He pushed off the counter.

"It isn't?" The look of surprise on her face shouldn't send fire shooting through his veins.

Dade bit his tongue rather than say something he'd regret.

"Stop. Don't tell me that I'm wrong. I always thought having money would make everything so much easier. If it doesn't, I'm not sure I want to know that just yet, considering I've spent my entire adult life trying to get a little of it." She held her ground. "With all the news surrounding me and my shop, I'm afraid everything I've been working toward will crumble into tiny pieces."

How the hell was Dade supposed to stay mad at that? Dade still hadn't figured out what his next move was going to be. Stay on the land he loved once the will was read? Or, get far away from all memories of Maverick Mike?

"Whatever happens can be put back together," he said.

"Easy for you to say." Disbelief darkened her eyes. When he really looked in them, there was something else sparkling, too. It looked a hell of a lot like desire, and that was another unproductive road.

"You think all I need for life to click into place is a last name?" He scoffed.

"I remember you in high school, Dade. You always had a group of people surrounding you, vying for your attention," she countered. "It wasn't like that for me."

Although he'd argue to the death that she had no idea what she was talking about when she hinted that life as a Butler was easy, she didn't need to hear that right now. She'd had a few really bad days strung together. Her shoulders were tense, her posture aggressive, and even though this was better than the look of defeat he'd seen in her eyes one too many times, he still wanted to ease her pain. There were dark circles from lack of sleep cradling her eyes. He took a step toward her.

Her pulse hammered, and he wasn't sure if it was from anger, frustration or desire. He ran his thumb across the base of her neck where he could feel her heart beat. "What happened to you after you left Cattle Barge?"

"Nothing." She looked up at him with defiance in her eyes. Talking could be overrated when it came to digging into emotional holes. Exactly the reason Dade preferred to keep his mouth shut. But he wanted to hear it from her instead of hearing it from the grapevine.

"Then why didn't we talk anymore when you came back?" he pressed as a mix of shock and horror flitted across her expression.

"Not you, too," she said.

"I'm your friend, Carrie. We used to tell each other everything," he shot back.

"I did talk." She glared at him.

"Not to me, you didn't." He stared deeper into her eyes, searching for something…desire? Permission?

"You weren't exactly lining up to have a conversation with me, either."

"I won't deny that. I wanted to talk to you, but I never got the vibe it was okay," he admitted.

"We were teenagers with hormones raging through our bodies. You were Mr. Popular Jock. I was an office aide because it was just too sad to work in the library. We didn't have anything in common once we started growing up." There was a hint of sadness in her voice but, again, it was better than defeat.

"I think we spent half our childhood on the tire swing. You remember that one on the playground?

It seemed so huge then. Saw it the other day and it looked different," he said, trying to break down a little of those stone walls.

"We grew up, Dade." All the warmth was gone from her expression now. "Our perspectives changed."

Damn if that wasn't true, even if chemistry pinged between them. Pure electricity and heat pulsed from her neck to his hand. He could tell she felt it by the way she stiffened for a split second every time they stood too close or their skin grazed. Don't get him started about the kisses they'd shared. He'd thought about those almost nonstop. So much fire. So much promise.

So much trouble.

She seemed intent on keeping him at arm's length, and after his last relationship, he had no plans to get involved with someone who wasn't into it. No matter how much his heart wanted to argue and say Carrie was exactly into it.

Carrie looked him right in the eye and said, "We should talk about something productive, like who might've killed Brett."

Her words had the effect of a slap across the cheek, jarring him back to reality. Dade dropped his hand. "I'll make coffee."

"Dade." Her sweet voice made him want to turn around. He missed the easy way she'd made him laugh.

"Yeah." He didn't turn around to face her. Instead, he paused at the doorway.

"I'm sorry. This whole ordeal has me turned up-side down, and I'm not sure if I'm coming or going anymore," she said. "That was really rude and you don't deserve to be treated like that, no matter how much stress I'm under."

"No need to apologize." He made quick work of the machine and produced two cups of coffee while she moved to the couch.

"This should help," he said.

She took the one being offered and thanked him. She was sitting on the sofa, her left leg curled underneath her bottom, and hugging a throw pillow. "My mind just keeps going in circles. Who would want Brett gone?"

"Who would benefit from his death?" He took a sip, remembering how it had tasted on her lips. *Great one, Dade. Way to leave it alone.*

"I keep asking myself the same question."

His cell phone buzzed. He checked the screen. "It's Ed."

"Sheriff Sawmill is requesting that Ms. Palmer voluntarily appear at the station to speak with him," Ed said.

"Why's that?" Dade had no plans to walk Carrie into a trap.

"He has a few questions. That's all he would disclose." Ed's voice was even.

"Does he plan to arrest her?" Dade asked.

"I asked the same question. He said no."

"What are her options?" Dade wanted to make sure he understood the situation correctly so that he could accurately relay the information to Carrie.

"She can refuse." Ed's voice was still even, and that was usually a good sign.

"But you wouldn't advise it," Dade said.

"Sheriff Sawmill gave me the impression he had news to share," Ed supplied.

Dade would stop short of trusting Sawmill, but he had complete faith in his attorney. "I'll take her in. Will you be there?"

Ed hesitated. "There's been a security violation at the ranch and Ella has asked me to stay here."

"What does that mean?" Dade dug his heels in and looked out the window. "What kind of violation?"

"It's under control now but a gentleman sprinted across the lawn and was then subdued by Terrell." Ed's words were reassuring. He had been the Mav's best friend and would want to make sure the family was safe. "Since the sheriff seems to view Ms. Palmer as a witness instead of a suspect, it's safe to say she's above suspicion for now. Will you escort her and let Terrell, Dalton and me take care of things here?"

"What happens on the ranch is my business." Guilt for neglecting his duties at home was a sucker punch to Dade's gut. None of his family would tell him that's what he'd been doing. He'd been working odd hours to keep up his part of family business. But

Dade's guilt wouldn't allow the cop-out. He could be doing more.

"Understood." Ed's voice was calm.

The problem was that being home made Dade think about his relationship with the Mav.

THE SHERIFF TOOK his usual spot across the expansive desk after ushering Carrie and Dade into his office. The ride over had been quiet, and Carrie wondered what was going on in Dade's mind. She could tell based on his expression that he was still stewing over the situation at the ranch. Ed had reassured him that everything was fine—no one had been hurt when a mentally challenged middle-aged man sprinted across the lawn with a knife in his hand. But right now her attention was on the sheriff.

"I sent the stuffed animal and the flower to the forensics lab. Mr. Staples apprised me of the situation, and I assure you that we're doing everything we can to find out who's targeting you," Sawmill began. His hands were folded on top of his desk. It sounded like his standard line, but at least Carrie didn't feel like a suspect anymore.

"Could someone want it to look like I murdered Brett?" she asked. "To throw your office off the trail?"

The sheriff paused thoughtfully. "That's an angle we're taking under consideration."

"But you don't think it's plausible," Dade interjected.

"Of course this is just my personal opinion—"

"Backed by twenty-five years of investigative experience," Dade added.

Sawmill nodded with a look of appreciation for the compliment.

"The person who committed this crime didn't come at it straightforward. Whoever it was wanted to avoid a personal confrontation, which is why he or she—" he glanced at Carrie with an apologetic look "—surprised the victim in the shower."

"Which means this person isn't strong enough to take Brett on," Dade said. "So, you're possibly looking at someone small in stature."

"That's the thinking. The initial reason Ms. Palmer fell under suspicion was because of her familiarity with the dog and her general size. Female perpetrators often don't attack a someone directly because of their weight and strength disadvantage."

Carrie was beginning to see a picture emerge. There were three women in Brett's life—her, his mother and his sister. None of them would do any harm to him, but at least she understood why she'd been questioned.

"The first thing we look for is motive," Sawmill supplied. His demeanor was softer this time, more cooperative.

"An argument in front of my store could hurt my business, and I've worked hard to be a success," she admitted.

Again, Sawmill nodded. "But those types of crimes usually occur in the heat of the moment, which didn't exactly add up, considering the victim in this case was murdered hours later."

"And one public disagreement wouldn't likely be enough to ruin what I have going," she added with a nod toward the sheriff.

"Right. So, we interviewed a few witnesses who stated that you were the one to end the relationship and that the victim didn't take it well." Another apologetic look in her direction, and she assumed it was for the invasion to her privacy.

"That's true. But what does that have to do with anything?" For the sake of finding Brett's actual killer, she could look past the intrusion, no matter how icky it felt to realize her life felt on display.

"In those cases, the person murdered is generally the one who broke off the relationship," Sawmill supplied.

Carrie didn't follow. "Why's that?"

"The jilted person can't stand the thought of the person he or she loves being with another man or woman, whichever being the case." Sheriff Sawmill leaned forward. "That's usually when things turn sour."

"Brett didn't want to break up. That was causing

a lot of friction between us," she supplied. But Sawmill would already know that based on the texts.

"I apologize for the question, but what happened? What was the reason you ended the relationship?" Sawmill asked.

"Honestly, the whole thing was a huge mistake on my part to begin with, and it didn't take long to realize. I'd been working too many hours at the ice cream shop and it was paying off professionally. Personally, not as much. My life had become nothing but work, and I decided to put myself back out there. Brett seemed nice enough in the beginning. I guess I liked the fact that he rode a motorcycle. It made him seem dangerous in a way. Reckless. He would come into the store and must've asked me out a dozen times before I finally agreed. Guess I knew all along that nothing would ever come of us." Admitting this in front of Dade made her uncomfortable, but she would do what it took to help the sheriff get on track to find the person who'd killed Brett.

"Was there an event that was the final straw? I'm curious as to what made you finally decide your relationship was over," the sheriff said.

Dade was studying the tile floor intently, and she couldn't get a feel for his reaction to what he was hearing. It seemed odd to be talking about her past relationship with him sitting next to her, but there was no reason it should. It wasn't like she and Dade were in a relationship. He was helping her sort out the mess that had become her life. He was being a good friend. And even though chemistry pinged between them, they both seemed to know acting on it would be a mistake. She would hurt him or vice versa.

"The writing was on the wall from the first date. We were too different. I mean, I thought we'd have something in common because we both grew up in tough circumstances," she said thoughtfully. "But I guess our reactions to that upbringing were totally off-kilter. He used his as an excuse to drink too much, to be a little too rude to people who were just trying to be nice. It was pretty obvious that we didn't look at the world in the same way."

"How long did the two of you go out?" The sheriff's gaze darted back and forth between Carrie and Dade.

"Longer than we should've. At first, it was nice to have someone to catch a movie with or eat dinner. We'd grab a drink after work. That lasted a few weeks before he surprised me by taking me to his family get-together. He said he wanted to go to the lake but he didn't tell me his mother and sister would be there. I freaked out and said I was sick and that I needed to leave. Then I started making excuses about having too much work. I let it drag out longer than I should've because I didn't want to hurt him. He was so into the relationship that I wanted to let him down softly." And she had a little guilt for letting the so-called relationship go on because she was tired of spending Friday nights alone.

"But he didn't agree." Sawmill picked up the Zantac packet but then tossed it down again, seeming to think better of taking one.

"No. He became even more convinced we should be together. Said he wanted to show me that we were meant to be and that I should give him a chance." Carrie crossed her legs and bounced her foot back and forth.

"And did you see things his way?"

"I told him that I needed a break in order to distract him and give him enough space to think clearly. My plan didn't work. He started trying to win me back. He texted almost constantly, which you've already seen, and left gifts at my business. He'd drive by to see if my car was in the parking lot when I said I was at work." Admitting how bad the relationship had become made her even more nervous about how it had ended. "I didn't mind parking in the back so he wouldn't know when I was there."

"And that's where Nash Gilpin found you the night you came in to file the complaint against him," the sheriff supplied.

Reality dawned. "I've considered that before, but the two of them couldn't have known each other, could they?"

"It's a connection we have to consider." The sheriff pinched the bridge of his nose, looking like he needed to stem a headache. He picked up the Zantac packet and ripped it open. "Which brings me back to the stuffed animal."

Reality hit with a hard smack. She felt like she might not be able to breathe if the sheriff was confirming her fear that Brett had been killed because of her. She couldn't help but think the dark cloud was extending to those she touched.

"Your ex keeps showing up, trying to win you back at the same time someone else is vying for your attention." The sheriff popped a Zantac in his mouth and took a swallow from the water bottle on his desk. "Nash had motive if he believed it was possible you'd get back together with Brett. Was Nash ever in your shop at the same time as Brett?"

"I'm not sure. I never really paid attention. Business was good before…all this started happening. The days would fly by." Carrie thought long and hard. How many times had Nash been in? Every day for two weeks. What times? He'd pop in throughout the day when he was on a break. "It's a definite possibility. In fact, I'm pretty sure he was there at least once at the same time as Brett, and it was a couple of days before the murder."

Dade turned to the sheriff. "Have you gotten any closer to locating Nash?"

Sawmill shook his head. "His employer gave us a couple of names of his next of kin, who we're currently trying to track down now. They're distant relatives so we're not hopeful. He doesn't exactly come from a stable family background, and it's most likely that he quit his job and moved on. The two events aren't necessarily related. The waterslide operator said Nash had been talking about making enough money to relocate to Florida. And that very well might be where he is. Until we locate him and have a conversation, he's at the top of our suspect list."

"From what you know about him already, does he fit the profile of a stalker?" Carrie asked.

"A guy who moves from town to town. Doesn't have many friends to speak of. It's possible. If this crime is romantically linked, a love-obsessed stalker is someone who would develop a fixation on a person he has no real personal relationship with. He would display some form of delusional behavior. Most of them suffer from a mental disorder."

Carrie's foot was making double time. "The guy did seem out of touch with reality, but I don't know about being delusional." She was no expert, but something had seemed off about him during the few times she'd interacted with him. She'd blamed it on alcohol but it could be more.

"One of his coworkers said he spent a lot of time alone, babbling about nothing in particular. Most of the people we spoke to knew about his drinking problem," the sheriff stated.

"What did his employer have to say about it?" Dade asked.

"The festival said they don't have funds to dig too deeply into every worker's background, because it's not uncommon to employ people who hop from job to job. He might have given them a fake Social Security number. Judge Watson subpoenaed the parent company's records first thing this morning. Funtimes Inc. has been ordered to give my office access to their files."

"And how did they respond?" Dade asked.

"We hope to know more in a few days when files arrive," the sheriff responded truthfully. "These things take time."

"Have you spoken to Samuel recently?" she asked.

The sheriff nodded.

"Is he okay?" She paused a beat. "He seemed really upset the night Nash cornered me. And then the next morning he stopped by the shop but Brett showed and I haven't seen Samuel since. Or Mrs. Hardin for that matter. Of course, I've been preoccupied so they could walk right past me and I might not realize it."

"He stopped by yesterday to find out if there were any leads in the case," the sheriff said.

Carrie leaned forward, unsure if she really wanted the answer to the question burning in the back of her mind about the investigation into Nash.

Did she have time to give?

Chapter Twelve

"What else can you tell us about a love-obsessed stalker?" Carrie wanted to know what she was up against.

"One of the key points to think about with a love-obsessed stalker is that he believes he can make the object of his affection love him, and that's where we believe the courtship is coming in with the stuffed animal and flowers." Sawmill flashed his eyes at Carrie. "Did Nash say anything to you that could give the impression he was obsessed?"

"He said I'd learn to love him a couple of times when he stopped by the shop." Carrie felt the blood rushing in her ears.

"This type of person would be desperate to develop a positive relationship with you," he added.

"I'm not so sure about that. He didn't seem to care if I wanted him around or not. In fact, he didn't seem to mind forcing himself on me."

Sawmill jotted down a couple of notes on the file

in front of him. "He would most likely have built an entire fantasy life of relationships with people he hardly knew."

"How far does this fantasy life go?" Carrie felt nauseous at the thought someone like that could be stalking her. All those times it had felt like eyes were watching her brought a chill to her spine.

"To the extent that he'd begin trying to act out his fictional plots in the real world," Sawmill supplied.

"Sounds like a crazy person," she shot back, rubbing the chill from her arms.

"A person like this is usually calculating. Deranged, yes. Crazy, no. The latter tends to be apprehended before any real crime has been committed based on a smaller offense," he supplied. "If we're dealing with what we think, in his mind, it's your fault that he has to do what he does."

"Is that because in his twisted mind I'm somehow responsible for his feelings toward me?" More chills assaulted her as the sheriff nodded.

"Which also tells me that he believes I'm asking for the attention in some way." Carrie swallowed the bile burning the back of her throat. "How far would this scenario be carried out? Say, for example, would this person kill his intended for her affection?"

"It's within reason," Sawmill said, and she could see that this wasn't any easier for him. He still hadn't solved the first high profile murder case on his desk, and crime had been multiplying in his county ever since. His reputation was on the line, and people were antsy. Her frustration at being treated like a suspect earlier dissolved a little bit more. All she could think about was bringing Brett's killer to justice and helping the sheriff catch the person who was obsessed with her.

"And at any point none of this seems wrong to the person?"

"Again, the person transfers that to the object of their obsession." Right. The sheriff had said that a few moments ago. "And what if Nash isn't responsible for Brett's death?" she asked. "Surely he can't be the only suspect. Did you check the couple of names I gave your deputy the other night?"

Sawmill said he had. "My deputies are dotting every i and crossing every t, interviewing everyone who might be connected. So far, we've gotten nothing on any of those leads. In the process, we've uncovered a few names to add to the list during our investigation, and we're hoping that you might be able to help us out by telling us if you've heard of any of these people."

Thinking about Brett had her also thinking about his dog, Tyson. Her heart fisted.

"Before we get into it, can I ask what's going to happen to Tyson?" she asked before the sheriff could continue. He must be scared now that his master was gone.

"Ms. Strawn didn't want him, so he's at the animal shelter." The sheriff shook his head.

"I'll take him," Dade said before Carrie could offer.

"From what I can see, he's not a very well-adjusted animal." Sawmill looked at Dade apologetically.

"Doesn't matter. We'll find a job for him on the ranch and train him. He'll be right as rain in no time." Carrie shouldn't allow her heart to swell at the gesture.

"I wish I could take him, but he's aggressive with other dogs and I have Coco," she offered.

"You can visit him any time you want, and within a couple of months Coco will be able to, as well." Dade's confidence in his ability to work with the animal was sexy, and Carrie's stomach gave a little flip. But then, he did own a ranch, or would when his father's will was read and had grown up around every kind of animal imaginable.

She smiled at Dade. A simple gesture, but it felt so right to be looking at him and smiling, even in the midst of all the craziness. It was probably just residual feelings from their childhoods, from a time when life was no more complicated than chasing each other around the playground in a game of tag. Just like it had felt right to kiss him, a little voice said, but she shut that down immediately. First of all, the thought couldn't be more inappropriate under the circumstances. And secondly…well…secondly didn't matter. The thought was inappropriate. Period.

"Sheriff, you said that you usually look at people close to the victim. Is there any chance his mother or sister could've been involved?" Although she couldn't imagine they would be. At this point she was throwing anything at the wall to see if it would stick.

"We're checking out his financials to see if there've been any recent changes," the sheriff said.

"And the names I supplied?" she asked again, reminding herself that thinking about Dade was as productive as trying to milk a chicken.

"Each had an alibi," he answered.

"What about his business?" Dade asked. "Any hint that there might've been trouble from there?"

"He'd been busy leading up to his murder. A pair of men who used to work for him have come forward to make a claim against his estate," the sheriff supplied.

"What right do they have?" Carrie couldn't help but come off as indignant at the thought of essentially grave robbers creeping out from all angles.

"They say they weren't paid for work they performed," the sheriff said.

"I might know who they are if you give me names," she offered.

"Ever hear Mr. Strawn talk about a man named Carl Buckley?" Sawmill asked.

Carrie searched her memory. She really wanted to help find the killer. But she came up empty. "He must've worked for Brett before we dated." Hearing the word *dated* seemed odd to her now. They'd barely been in a relationship to begin with and now she was trying to help find Brett's killer. It was surreal, but life had taught her to expect the worst and she should've known better than to get too comfortable. Everything had been going a little too well before all this started and she blamed herself for getting involved with Brett in the first place. That sounded horrible now that he was gone, but it was true. She should never have agreed to go against her better judgment and date him. And he could be dead because of their relationship if someone had killed him because of an obsession with her.

The sheriff picked up the packet of Zantac and stuffed it in his shirt pocket. "Buckley's pretty well known around town for his drinking. He doesn't have a reliable track record of showing up to work at previous jobs."

"If he was late too often or showed up drunk on the job, Brett would've fired him right then and there. He wouldn't have put his men or livelihood at risk." Carrie shook her head. "His strict policy might've made the guy angry if he felt justified."

"There's another gentleman by the name of Dave Lancaster," Sawmill stated.

"I know who he is." She didn't have to dig deep

into her memories for that one. His carelessness had made him unpopular on job sites. "He was an OSHA nightmare fully realized. I remember Brett said he was careless. He'd drop tools from scaffolding and not shout a heads-up for anyone who might be walking below. Brett didn't like to use him. I can't remember how many times Brett said Dave was going to kill someone if he couldn't toe the line."

"How did others on the job site react to his behavior?" Sawmill asked.

"They didn't like Dave at all. Some of the guys threatened to quit if Brett didn't get things under control." She rocked her foot back and forth, figuring the sheriff was no closer to figuring this out than she was.

"Were there any threats made to Brett?" Sawmill quirked a brow, and she could almost see the wheels turning in his head. At the very least, this information seemed to change things for him—hopefully it would get him closer to finding out who had killed Brett. Yes, Nash was a possibility, but he was feeling more like a long shot to Carrie. What would his real motive be?

"Nothing that he shared with me." *Oh. Wait. Hold on.* "Hector was hurt by one of Dave's actions. He left some tool lying around on the ground that Hector stepped on—maybe a nail gun?—and whatever it was shot a nail right through his foot. Hector made all kinds of threats in the heat of the moment, but

Brett didn't take it too seriously. He said Hector would cool down and come around."

"And he fired Dave after that?" Sawmill's brow shot up.

"He must've. I don't know for certain. Things had already started to unravel between us, and I was trying to get him to give me space when he was going through all of that," she admitted.

"Did you ever meet Hector Reglan?" Sawmill asked.

"Not face-to-face, no. But I felt like I knew him, because Brett talked about how Hector's wife would make homemade tamales for the guys on Fridays if they'd had a good week." Carrie had wanted to love someone enough to want to cook for his coworkers. "They have two kids."

"And his wife never brought them to your shop?" Sawmill seemed to catch onto this last bit of information.

"Not once. I think money was tight and she didn't want the kids to get used to spending money on things they could make at home." She paused. "I offered to treat them, but Brett said Hector would be too proud to accept, so I left it alone."

"I'll talk to Hector and his wife. See where they were on the night of the murder." Sawmill took down a few notes. "What about his neighbors? Was he close to any of them?"

"If you're asking if he knew them well enough

for one of them to walk right past Tyson, then no," she stated. "Brett was having trouble with one of his neighbors."

The sheriff perked up.

"They were having fights over messes he was leaving in the front yard. His work truck was old and he parked it out front. She called and had it towed a few times. I never met her and she might've been justified in her complaints, but I forgot to mention her before."

"Which side?" Sawmill asked.

"She's to the right. I don't know her name." She gave a helpless shrug. Based on his line of questioning, she was becoming more certain that he was digging around for possibilities.

"What about ex-girlfriends?" Sawmill continued. "He talk about any bad blood there?"

"Regina Kastle—with a *K*—kept texting him long after the breakup," she supplied.

"Did he say what she wanted?" Sawmill asked.

"Money, mostly. She had a baby, and I think he was helping her out financially while they dated." She shook her head. "I didn't know anything about this until close to the end of our relationship. In fact, she was another in a long list of reasons Brett and I weren't a good match from the beginning. He kept too many secrets."

"Was the baby his?" the sheriff asked.

"I don't think so," she said. "They started dating when her little girl was already six months old."

"And he didn't tell you any of this right away?" Sawmill asked.

"Are you married?"

Sawmill nodded.

"Really? How long?" she asked.

He quirked a brow but played along. "Twenty-two years."

"Congratulations," she offered. "That's a long time."

He was quick to nod.

"You remember much about those early days of dating? When everything was new?" she asked.

"Most of it. Sure," Sawmill admitted.

"Did Mrs. Sawmill tell you everything about every guy she'd dated during those first few dates?" Carrie asked.

Sawmill's hands were already up in surrender. "No, she did not. In fact, she'd dated one of my best friends the year before and I didn't know about it until right before our wedding, when she confessed. Said holding in the secret was making her sick and that she'd understand if I didn't want to go through with the wedding."

"So I'm guessing you already know the answer to your question," she said.

"Yes, ma'am. I believe that I do." Sawmill repositioned in his seat. "I've seen the line out the door of your shop."

"Not anymore. All the media attention I've been getting is going to run me out of business," she stated with a little more heat than she'd intended.

"I'm sorry to hear that." The sheriff seemed sincere. "My wife can't get enough of your Vanilla Bean-illa."

"Most people love that one." She smiled, but it didn't reach her eyes. "I'd be happy to have a batch ready if you want to stop by after work."

"I'm curious," he continued without answering, "how do you get the flavors just right? I mean, I've eaten a lot of ice cream in my day." He patted his stomach, which admittedly was a little big. "I'm normally a home-style vanilla guy, but the vanilla in yours makes my old one seem…" He paused. "I don't know, lacking in some way."

"Practice, Sheriff Sawmill. That's how I perfected the recipe. I spent a few weeks on that recipe alone and I had to have the vanilla shipped in." She was proud of the care she took in developing each recipe.

"Then you understand what it means to be thorough. I have to ask questions. Even the ones I know the answers to in advance. I ask anyway because it's my job and every once in a while—not often, mind you, maybe a handful of times in twenty-five years—someone surprises me with a different answer and a case is solved out of what feels like thin air." He clasped his hands together and placed them on top of the desk.

Dade stood. "If there's nothing else Carrie can help you with, I'd like to take her home."

"I'll take you up on the ice cream sometime," he said to Carrie.

"Anytime, Sheriff. Don't be shy."

And somehow she had a feeling he was going to take her up on that offer.

Chapter Thirteen

"Can you drop me off at work in a few hours?" Carrie asked Dade as she let Coco in the back door of her home. It was almost dark, and she didn't want to risk leaving her car anywhere near the shop for the reporters to see it. "I'll take her in with me."

"There are a few things I need to take care of at the ranch," Dade supplied. "Will you be okay if I don't stick around after I drop you?"

"Of course." The thought of Nash running around loose somewhere didn't do great things to Carrie's stress levels. Focusing on work would take her mind off everything going on, and especially all the confusing feelings she had toward Dade.

A truck engine roared next door, and gravel spewed underneath tires on the drive.

"Guess my neighbor's finally home," she said. "He made a big deal out of my trash blowing into his yard. Cursed me out the other day."

"What's his name?" Dade asked. The look on his face said he wasn't thrilled.

"I'm not sure." She shrugged. "I tried to go over a couple of times when I saw his truck was parked out front. I know he was there, but he didn't answer the door. And then I was letting Coco out the other night and he came home yelling across the yard for me to keep my trash on my side. I tried to explain that it was probably raccoons, but he didn't want to hear any of it."

"When did he move in?" Dade asked.

"Around six months ago, I think. He's almost never home, though." Carrie couldn't contain the frustration in her voice.

"Maybe I should have a talk with him," Dade said, his tone indicating he'd be doing most of the talking.

"Don't worry about it. He's a jerk," she said. "He's not worth the energy."

Speaking of neighbors, the mail carrier had mistakenly put a piece of Samuel's aunt's mail in Carrie's box. She hadn't seen either of them lately, but then, she'd been consumed with her own problems. She remembered making a note to drop off ice cream the other day. Another thing that had fallen off her radar.

Her life felt like it was slipping through her fingers lately. And there was no way to catch hold and take back control, no matter how much she tried.

The deep ridges in Dade's forehead said he was determined to defend her. She already had bad relations with her neighbor, and she didn't want to make things worse.

"Promise me you'll leave it alone." She looked into Dade's eyes and almost faltered when he studied her. "I already have more going on than I can handle."

And then his stone features softened. "What happened?"

"I already told you," she said.

"I don't mean with him." He gestured toward next door.

It dawned on her what he was talking about. She lifted her shoulder as casually as she could. "It was a long time ago. Doesn't matter now."

Dade took a tentative step toward her. "It does to me."

If she opened up that dam, there'd be no way to handle the flooding. Part of her wanted to let go, to finally talk to someone about it, but she couldn't. It was too hard. Tears burned the backs of her eyes. Just thinking about it brought a heavy cloak around her shoulders.

"Carrie." The softness in his voice, the compassion made it hard to breathe.

She needed to do something to change the subject before her ribs cracked and her chest exploded.

"I need a shower."

By THE TIME Dade picked Carrie up from the shop the next day, exhaustion had set it. The thought of losing the business she'd worked so hard for sat heavy in her chest. The stabbing pain in her left shoulder blade had intensified.

After greeting Dade, she coaxed Coco onto the seat, where the Sharp Eagle perched in the center.

Dade's expression was intense. Deep grooves were carved in his forehead, and worry lines underlined his serious blue eyes. His jaw clenched as he turned the steering wheel, guiding them out of the alley.

"Everything okay?"

"There's a lot going on with my family, a lot of media," he said. "I'm sorry they've picked up on me helping you."

"Don't be, because I'm not. I'm grateful for everything you've been doing for me, Dade."

She liked that the muscle in his jaw released some of its tension when he half smiled.

"You're welcome," he said. She liked making him feel better, even if she wasn't ready to tell him everything.

"I keep mulling over the possibilities of who could have killed Brett," he said.

"Same with me," she admitted, leaning her head against the seat and rubbing her temples. "I still can't fathom anyone wanting him gone, and especially not because of me. Look, I know he wasn't always the nicest guy and I realized my mistake in dating him. But no one deserves this."

"I'd like to speak to Nash," Dade said.

"Me, too. I just wish he'd turn up somewhere. I feel like he holds the key to what we're looking for, and it's beyond frustrating that no one can locate him." She gripped her cell. There were no messages on it. Not like her last phone. This one was quiet, and it was a strange feeling. "I've been thinking about what's next for me. Sales are dwindling, and it's only a matter of time before I have no customers left."

"People are skittish right now. The town's been through a lot recently. It'll settle down, and you'll be able to open your doors again when people forget," Dade reassured. "And they will."

"Have you forgotten about my past?" Carrie scoffed. What if they didn't forget? She had to think about an exit strategy. She had a little money saved. Maybe she could move to Austin and start a new business. It would only be a matter of time before she'd run out of money at this location. Eric and Harper were still on Carrie's payroll, coming in overnight to help with mail orders. She'd managed to get her dairy and dry goods vendors to send deliveries earlier in the morning. Her staff had assured her they'd work whatever hours she could give and she felt responsible for their jobs. She'd take a pay cut if she had to in order to keep them employed. There were the reporters outside her house—a place that felt even less like home now. Which reminded her, she needed to let Samuel know what was going on.

He must be wondering why she suddenly had security at her house.

"I can probably guess what you're thinking right now." Dade broke through the thoughts spiraling her to a pit of hopeless.

"Then tell me, because I feel like I'm all over the place." She blew out a frustrated breath.

"What city are you considering?" he asked as he waved to Adam, the security guard working the overnight shift. Dade had made a point of having photos of each guard sent to him as an extra precaution.

Dade pulled into her driveway.

Her neighbor's truck was parked on the pad next to his house.

"I wasn't—"

Dade shot her a look.

"Austin," she relented. "How'd you know?"

"We've been friends a very long time." He put a lot of emphasis on the word *friends*. Was that because he didn't want her to confuse his kindness for something else? The few kisses they'd shared held a lot more heat than a friendly gesture. But she figured that he was reminding himself as much as her that the two of them trying to be anything but friends was worse than a bad idea.

She didn't figure this was the time to remind him that they'd been childhood pals and nothing more. They'd gone their separate ways in high school and certainly didn't run in the same circles then or now.

Seeing him in the alley the other night was the most they'd talked since they were kids. So how did he think he knew her?

He might've made a lucky guess, but Dade had no idea what was really running through her mind or he would've hightailed it in the other direction a long time ago.

Carrie got out of the truck. "Come on, Coco."

Stubbornly, Coco went out the driver's side at Dade's heels.

"She probably smells Flash on me," he said by way of explanation.

"Who's that?" Carrie unlocked the front door, ignoring her frustration that even her dog liked Dade more than she liked her owner.

Dade followed Carrie, and her heart gave a little flip because her emotions were so mixed up, so confused that they had her wanting to reach for comfort in his arms.

"I changed Tyson's name," he supplied. "We're giving him a fresh start with his life, and he needed a new name to go with it."

"That's a great idea. I like the name." She wished the messes in her life could be untangled so easily. "How'd he respond to the change?"

"He adapted right away."

"What made you give him the name Flash?" She was curious as to his thinking.

"That's all it takes to change." Dade snapped his fingers. "And Split Second was too long."

She laughed despite the heavy feelings weighing her down.

Change? She wished she knew that trick, because her past had always haunted her. She felt like a slave to a life she'd worked so damn hard to get away from.

Dade took a step toward her, and she backed up a few steps until her back touched the door. He looked so far into her eyes that she felt like he could see right through to her toes. "Don't go away again, Carrie," he said and his voice was low and gravelly. Sexy.

With those intense blue eyes staring into hers, she'd be willing to promise just about anything. Except that she'd stick around.

"If I lose my business, there'll be nothing left for me here." Her voice shook with uncertainty.

"You won't." He was so confident even as hurt flashed in his eyes.

She wished she shared his opinion, that she could believe it was true from deep down and not somewhere on the surface where it could be pulled under. *She* could be pulled under.

His gaze dropped to her lips, and her throat went dry.

"Do you plan to kiss me or stand there and stare at me all night?" she asked with as much bravado as she could, which was saying a lot. With his strong male presence toe to toe with her, she could feel masculinity pulse from him, and it made her legs weaken. Afraid they might not be able to carry her weight, she braced herself against the wall behind her and tugged his face down to meet hers.

He took in a deep breath a half second before their lips crashed together. Hunger rolled off him in tangible waves. Electricity hummed through her as the kiss deepened.

With his mouth moving against hers, she got lost…lost in his touch as his hands cupped her face… lost in his clean masculine scent. He was all outdoors and male and strength.

Before she could debate her actions, her hands went to the hem of his T-shirt. He helped her by shrugging out of it, and then she unbuttoned her blouse. Her shirt joined his on the floor next to them as he cupped her breasts in his hands. They swelled and pressed against the lace of her bra. Her nipples beaded as his thumbs rolled over them and a low raspy breath poured from his mouth.

She undid her bra, needing to feel skin against skin. Hunger burned through her as his strong hands grazed her skin. His touch was light at first, causing need to swell inside her, overtaking every rational thought that this might be a bad idea.

"You're beautiful, Carrie. You've always been beautiful," he said in that low, gravelly voice that sent sensual ripples skittering across her skin.

All that did was fan the flames burning inside her.

Need overtook logic again when her hands flew to his zipper. She helped him shed his jeans and boxers, and there was just enough light in the room to show the ripples of his abs, the patch of dark hair trailing south from his belly button.

Carrie was out of her shorts and lacy underwear in two seconds flat and he groaned other words of appreciation for her body. She doubted that she was beautiful in reality, but he made her feel like she was. She should be embarrassed, standing there naked and exposed in front of Dade, but it felt as natural as the sun shining.

She realized that she'd wanted this, to be with him, for longer than she cared to let herself remember or admit.

Her arms wound around his neck as he lifted her off her feet easily. Their lips found each other's as he made his way to the bedroom. She could feel his thick length pulsing against her skin. Her stomach gave a little flip, and she pressed her lips to his even harder. She needed this—him.

In the next second she was on the bed and his strong body was on top of her, pressing her into the mattress.

She reached for the nightstand next to her bed and felt around for a condom. She held it up to him and he ripped it open before she helped him roll it onto his silky length. She stretched her fingers around his erection, and he made another guttural groan of pleasure.

"Carrie." More sensual skitters flitted across her skin when he said her name. She could get used to the sound on his lips. She loved the way he tasted, minty and like he'd just had a cup of coffee. And he probably had.

This should feel strange, but it didn't. Being with Dade seemed like the most natural thing. She brought her hands up to his neck and tunneled her fingers into his hair as he dipped his tip inside her. A battlefield of sensation lit as he teased himself deeper and deeper toward her core.

It didn't take long for him to bring her to the edge of ecstasy as he threaded her nipples between his thumb and forefinger. His tongue inside her mouth built to a fever pitch.

Carrie matched him, stride for stride, as need climbed to impossible heights. And just before she let go and flew off the cliff with him, free-falling toward the earth at a dizzying pace, she thought she heard Dade whisper, "I love you."

Chapter Fourteen

Dade stirred, instinctively reaching for Carrie. All he felt was cold sheets next to him. He untangled himself and checked the clock on the nightstand. Three thirty a.m. He pushed off the bed and glanced around. Light from down the hall made it easy enough to locate his boxers, which had been folded and placed on top of a neat pile on the chair next to the door. His boots were tucked underneath.

He threw on his boxers and jeans and headed out to find her.

"Hey," she said as he emerged from the hall. She sat on a chair near the front window with her legs tucked underneath her sweet round bottom. Her hand was at her face, and it looked like she was chewing on her nail.

"What's wrong?" He strode across the room and bent down to kiss her.

"Nothing." She turned her head in time for him to catch her cheek instead of her lips. Whoa. What the hell did that mean? She'd put on the brakes awfully quick.

"Seriously, what's going on?" He needed something from her, some kind of sign to know what had happened between them was okay. A few hours ago had changed everything. He'd hoped she felt the same.

She smiled up at him, but it didn't reach her eyes. She grabbed his forearm. "I'm sorry. I don't mean to be distracted. I've just been thinking."

There was an empty coffee mug next to her, indicating she'd been awake for a while. Had she gone to sleep at all after they'd made love? He'd been out pretty quick after what he'd thought was the best sex of both of their lives. Now, he felt a little insecure. He almost laughed out loud at the thought. Dade Butler had never had an insecure moment when it came to his love life in the past.

This must have something to do with his relationship with his father. Recently, the Mav had been making an effort and Dade had shot his father down, confused over the timing. Hell, why now? After all these years, why had his father suddenly wanted to have a different relationship? It had all been pretty clear-cut before. The Mav did his own thing and his children did theirs. The only common thread was that everyone deeply cared about the ranch, the land and—at least in the case of his kids—each other.

Not being able to find out why the Mav had had

a change of heart now that he was gone was eating away at Dade's resolve. He could admit that—and it was most likely why Carrie's rejection stung so much.

"I need coffee. Want some?" he asked as he turned toward the kitchen.

"I've had enough," she said.

He returned a couple of minutes later with a new perspective following a little bit of a caffeine boost. He took a seat on the couch across the room from Carrie. She looked exhausted, and a moment of guilt hit that he'd kept her awake when she should've been sleeping. It was probably his pride turning her rejection over and over again in his head. That and the fact that Dade hadn't been rejected much in his life. Wounded pride had him feeling like this was a bigger deal than it was. Sure, they'd had great sex. His body got going again just thinking about how silky her skin felt against his hands. *Way to keep things light, Butler.*

"What's keeping you from sleep?" He sure as hell hoped she wasn't about to say the fact that he was in her bed.

Coco hopped up on the couch next to him and settled down.

"A few thoughts keep rolling around in my head, and I can't seem to let them go," she said.

He waited as she gathered her thoughts, taking a sip of coffee to get his own mental engines revved up.

"Do you remember the profile the sheriff gave of the kind of person who could be watching me?" she asked.

"Sawmill said something about a loner. He would most likely suffer from a mental disorder," he supplied.

"I was so sure that it was Brett leaving those 'gifts' on my car and here at home. I know that summer dress was here." In going through all the possible suspects, she could cross one name off the list, and that was her ex. It was obvious to Dade that she couldn't even begin to process the guilt that had her convinced his death was somehow her fault. "And then I started looking at everyone differently. Could it have been someone I knew? Eric or Teddy the delivery guy?"

"Eric definitely doesn't fit the profile. Sawmill said he had a girlfriend who vouched for him. He has no criminal history and hangs out with quite a few friends on the weekends. He plays on a recreational volleyball team and volunteers to coach in his church league," Dade reminded her.

"I know. The profile of a stalker is quite the opposite. The person the sheriff is looking for probably has a mental disorder, which could be difficult to detect if the person was good at hiding it. He most likely spends most of his time alone and doesn't have friends. The sheriff also said that he suffers from delusional thought patterns and behaviors, and that brings me to Nash." She crossed her legs and started rocking her foot.

"We don't know as much about him. The fact that he doesn't have roots anywhere doesn't necessarily make him a stalker. But then, his lifestyle of moving around and not really making any friends could put him in that category," Dade continued. "And we don't even know where he is."

"He could be anywhere," she said with a visible shudder.

"Including Canada by now for all we know."

"True." She stared out the front window. "Or right here under our noses."

"He hasn't been seen in town," he reassured her.

"Another good point. But what if it's not him? So far, he's the only person I keep coming back to. But what if it's someone else? I mean, he's a drunk. Does that fit the profile? He was sloppy, too. And that gets me thinking that it might not be him. The sheriff is still digging around for suspects. I'm starting to wonder who else it could be." She looked out the window toward her neighbor's house with that blank, defeated expression that Dade had come to hate. "I have no idea who my neighbor is, and I've never once seen someone visit. From all that I can tell, he's a loner and he could have a disorder. He keeps odd hours, and who knows what he's really doing when he's gone for days on end. He snapped at me when I tried to speak to him the other day. Maybe us being nice to each other is not in the fantasy world he created if it's him."

Dade moved to the window. He didn't want to acknowledge the sting of rejection he felt that intensified the closer he was to her. "There's a light on at his house. Maybe it's time he and I get to know each other a little better."

She reached out and touched his arm. More of those frustrating frissons of heat zinged through him, and especially at the thought she didn't feel the same. The sexual chemistry was obvious, but he wanted more than one night.

"Be careful," she warned.

CARRIE SAT IN the chair, looking out the front window. Making love to Dade had thrown her completely off balance. Her world had tilted on its axis.

To make matters worse, she'd thought he'd said he loved her. Everything inside her wanted to believe those three words, to believe that the fantasy could come true and that she and Dade could have a future together.

But then she remembered everyone she'd lost and she would lose him, too. Loving Dade would mean opening herself up to unimaginable pain if he walked away. And that was the problem. She couldn't allow herself to open that vein again. Not even with Dade.

When this whole ordeal was over, and it would be at some point, she would have to be okay with leaving Cattle Barge. It hadn't turned out to be the welcoming home she'd been searching for when she'd opened the shop last year.

Maybe she would never feel like she was home anywhere. A little voice in the back of her mind said she was home when she was with Dade. She wouldn't argue against it because she'd be wasting her time.

But she didn't have to give in to the feeling, either.

Whatever it took, Carrie had to protect herself even if it meant shutting out the one man she could see herself loving for the rest of her life.

Chapter Fifteen

Dade gave the door a couple of taps. The light inside the bungalow-style house turned off. *Come on. Don't be a jerk.*

Dade intended to have a conversation with the man. He needed to feel him out and get a read on the guy.

A few more taps, harder this time, and there was no sign of movement. Obviously, the guy was home. Dade's blood pressure spiked as he turned away, resigned to speak to the man another time.

The door swung open fast and an intense-looking man a few inches shorter than Dade stepped forward in a threatening manner. Well, it would be threatening to someone smaller and weaker than Dade. The second his eyes sized up Dade, the guy's posture instantly changed.

"Hey, sorry. I thought you were someone else," he said with his hands up, palms out toward Dade in the surrender position.

"Do you mean like your next-door neighbor?" Dade kept his feet positioned in an athletic stance.

"Not her in particular, but women in general," he snapped.

Didn't that boil Dade's blood pressure? The guy might not be intimidating to Dade, but he would be to someone smaller than him. And this creep might be trying to scare Carrie.

"And what exactly do you have against women?" Dade fisted and released his hands at his sides.

"How long do you have to hear about it?" The joke fell flat. He stuck out his hand, a peace offering. "I'm Kyle, by the way."

"Dade Butler." He took the outstretched hand after a pause and realized Kyle's hand was shaky. Did he have something to hide? Or was he afraid of Dade?

"Sorry about before." Kyle looked to be a few years older than Dade, but not by much. "My mind's been in a bad place since the divorce."

The last word tipped Dade into a new direction. Being divorced could make Kyle angry toward women. Although Sawmill had said stalkers were usually single. To be fair, this guy was single now, but loners didn't usually get married in the first place. Although, there were always exceptions. Dade remembered that a notorious serial killer from Kansas had been married with kids.

"Come in." Kyle motioned.

Going inside would give Dade a chance to check out the place. See if there was anything suspicious.

Dade thanked him as he stepped inside. Kyle closed the door.

"You want a beer or something? I don't sleep well anymore and having a beer calms my mind." Kyle's living room consisted of a couch and a flat screen that had been mounted to the wall. There was a Blu-ray player on the floor. A sound bar had been placed on top of a book. Other than that, there were kids' toys spilling out of an opened chest with a cartoon print on it.

"No, thanks. I'm waking up, not winding down," he replied.

"Mind if I have one?" Kyle asked.

"Nope." Dade followed him into the kitchen. There wasn't much to the decor, but the place had all the necessities and was neat enough.

"Butler," Kyle repeated, popping open the top of a can of brew. "I've heard that name before."

"My family owns a pretty big cattle ranch around here," Dade offered, not wanting to go into the details of the Mav's murder—and most likely the real reason Kyle had heard the name—with a stranger. Dade could admit that his emotions were heightened with everything that had been going on in his family.

Kyle nodded.

"What's your problem with Carrie?" Dade asked outright.

"Who?" Kyle looked genuinely surprised.

Dade motioned toward her house. "Your neighbor."

"Oh." Recognition dawned. He shot another apologetic look. "I guess I've been a jerk to her. To just about everyone since the divorce."

"That what brought you to Cattle Barge?" Dade asked. Anyone new in town was suspect to him after everything that had happened, was still happening. And that wasn't exactly fair.

"It was as far away as I could get from my ex and her family in Austin without putting too much distance between me and my son," he admitted. He sounded angry when he mentioned his ex. Dade could feel ripples of annoyance pulsing from Kyle, and his thinned lips gave away his attitude toward his ex. Toward women?

"Bad divorce?" he asked casually.

"That's putting it lightly." Kyle located his phone and pulled up a pic of a smiling kid with a round face who looked like a younger version of the man standing next to Dade. "But my son is nothing like his mother. He's seven."

The guy's posture changed when he spoke about his child. His face lit up, and the worry lines etched in his forehead eased. "She's taking me to court again, trying to get full custody."

That kind of anger toward one woman could translate to others, right?

"That's a tough break." Dade had seen firsthand the damage when a relationship went sour. If that's all there was to this, Kyle would be in the clear.

"I lost my job because of her father. He owned part of the company I worked at. Had me fired when I refused to give up my son." There was so much venom in the guy's expression now. This seemed to go a little deeper than a father's love for his child— there was a bigger story behind this kind of hatred. But it did offer a plausible explanation as to why the guy would want to close out the rest of the world. The thing Dade couldn't reconcile was, wouldn't the guy want revenge on his ex?

"Cute kid," Dade said.

"He's my world," Kyle admitted, and there was so much love and admiration in his voice that Dade believed it. "But she almost cost me that, too, planting ideas in his head about me."

"I can see why you'd need a minute to reboot," Dade stated. He couldn't help but think about his own situation with his father. Had the Mav ever loved his kids as much?

"I don't always know the right things to say or do, but I'd do anything for that kid." Kyle drained the beer and crunched the can in his fist. "I came here for a fresh start, but that witch won't leave me alone. She already has everything—our house, our dog, our son for most of the time. And that's not enough for Daddy's spoiled princess. She wants me to disappear. I should never have married up. I was out of my league and had no idea what the fallout would be when she didn't get her way."

"Sorry to hear it. That's rough on you and has to be hard on the kid, too. It's obvious you love him." Dade couldn't believe he was about to say that making mistakes seemed par for the course for a parent. And yet a nagging voice said it was true.

"Liam's the best kid. He doesn't deserve any of this, and especially not the way I yelled at him a few weeks ago. The pressure of everything has been getting to me. He dropped a glass of milk by accident and I went off," Kyle said, and there was so much torment in his eyes.

A former father-in-law with money who was used to giving everything to his little princess wouldn't take any of this well. Dade had enough experience with powerful men to realize how much they were used to getting their way and how determined they could be to bend another's will.

A court battle and a woman hell-bent on waging war could make anyone a little crazy, and especially with a child involved. Could it make Kyle want to lash out at all women?

"Do you live next door?" Kyle asked. "I haven't seen you around, but then I'm not here much."

"Carrie's a good friend of mine. We've known each other since we were little kids."

Kyle's eyes narrowed. "Always starts out that way, before they get your heart, and then you're not the man either one of you thought you were when they trample all over you."

Kyle had suffered a bad breakup, was deep into a fight for his child. But that brought up a good point. Would he risk losing the kid?

"What are you doing for work?" Dade asked, wondering if that had anything to do with his coming and going at odd hours.

"Anything I can." He shook his head. "Mostly construction jobs here and there around Texas." That could explain why the guy kept an odd schedule. "The crazy thing is that the judge wants me to show consistent income, and I need that in order to pay child support. But my ex's father is doing everything he can to keep me blacklisted from working as an accountant, where I could make a decent living."

"Tough situation," Dade agreed.

"They haven't heard the last of me." Kyle banged his fist on the counter. "I won't give up on being in my son's life. He's not happy with me right now, and I messed that up. I should've been calmer and handled the whole situation better."

Dade had to admit that he felt a certain tug toward believing the guy based on his passion for his kid. All parents should be so dedicated. But he was trying to keep his personal feelings out of it and look at the situation objectively, for Carrie's sake.

"Sorry about your situation," Dade said, watching for his reaction.

"I'll figure it out," Kyle said.

"Next door. She's been through a lot and deserves a break."

Kyle's posture tensed. "Guess I've been too caught up in my own mess to think much about anyone else. You could say that I've been a class-A jerk to pretty much everyone around me."

"A bad relationship can do that." Dade was satisfied that Kyle wasn't a threat. He made a move toward the front door.

"Thanks for stopping by. I haven't really talked to anyone in months," Kyle admitted. "Guess I've been holed up here, licking a few wounds."

Dade understood constructing walls. He was starting to see the cost of them, too. Those same walls keeping him safe would shut everyone else out. Construct them high enough and he'd never be able to see over them.

"Easy to see why," Dade stated.

"I don't want to be *that* guy who everyone sees coming and crosses the road to avoid. I figured it would be better if I just kept to myself completely." Worry lines creased Kyle's forehead and bracketed his mouth. "I used to be pretty social before all this—" he glanced around "—before my life was held up in court and waiting for visitation while trying to pull together enough scratch to make my child support payments and keep a roof over my own head. Once this nightmare is over, I should get out more.

I had no idea how difficult it would be to move to a new city and go back and forth to see my son."

"It can't be easy," Dade agreed, figuring Kyle was spilling his guts because he hadn't had anyone to talk to in a long time. He'd isolated himself and Dade was even more grateful for the love and support of his brother and sisters. They kept him from going too far and vice versa.

"You wouldn't believe how much my soon-to-be ex freaked out when I took Liam fishing. She said that I violated my visitation and called me a flight risk. Me. I'm a guy who grew up in Austin and only left to move to San Antonio to be closer to her family after college." That deep well of anger surfaced every time he spoke about his ex. "She got a court order for supervised visitation, complaining that I took him out of town without permission. It's been too easy to stay under the radar, and especially with everything that's been going on. I should've gotten the hell out of that relationship when my future in-laws started telling us when and where we'd go on vacation." He flashed his eyes at Dade. "I'm not exactly the roll-over-on-command type, and my marriage was affected. Eventually, it cracked, then broke, but I got a great kid out of it."

"Sounds worth it to me." For the first time, Dade thought about having a family of his own. The notion of having his own child hit him.

"Yeah, I guess I've had one focus for the past few

months," he admitted. "But, hey, is everything okay next door?"

"She's had a rough go lately," Dade stated. "Have you seen anyone hanging around, looking in her windows?"

"Now I really feel like a jerk for the other night." Kyle rubbed the day-old scruff on his chin. "I ripped into her for her trash getting into my yard. I owe her an apology for that."

"She mentioned it." Dade shot a warning look and Kyle acknowledged.

"No, I haven't seen anyone around, but then, I'm probably not the right guy to ask. I've been keeping my head down and sticking to my own business," Kyle admitted.

"Someone's been leaving her unwelcome gifts, like a rose on her back porch and a stuffed animal out front." Dade specifically mentioned the items to see if the guy flinched. One little twitch could give away if a person was lying. Kyle's body language didn't change, which gave Dade the impression the guy didn't know anything as Dade had already suspected.

"This person make threats or is he just leaving her stuff?" Kyle's brow shot up.

Fair question. "Someone's keeping tabs on her."

"That's pretty creepy, if you ask me." Kyle's posture tensed. The horrified look on his face gave Dade the impression this was all news to him.

"She's not liking the attention, but the guy won't

show his face, so she has no idea who he is," Dade continued. "Her ex had been harassing her and something happened to him."

"Like what?" Kyle seemed genuinely shocked when it dawned on him. "He was murdered?"

Dade nodded.

"Damn." He rubbed that scruff again. "I had no idea any of this was going on. I feel like an even bigger jerk. Guess it's time to pick my head up and out of the sand and be a better man."

Kyle said all the right words. Dade could admit it, and some of them even hit him in an unexpected place and got him thinking about his own actions with his father.

"What can I do to help?" Kyle asked.

"Let me know if you see anything suspicious going on at her place." With everything going on he figured Carrie would be safer at the ranch. If he could talk her into it, and that was a big if.

The two exchanged cell information.

Getting her to agree to stay with him at his place was going to be his second order of business for the day. "She might not be around much, so I'd appreciate a second pair of eyes on her place."

"Yeah, man, whatever I can do. When I'm home I'll make sure no one's hanging around or bothering her," he said.

Loud barks cut through the air. The owner was unmistakable as another round fired off. Coco.

Dade glanced from Kyle to the back door.

"Go out this way. It's faster," Kyle said. "I'll come with you."

Dade was already gunning toward the door. "Call the sheriff."

Chapter Sixteen

Dade's heart threatened to explode at the thought of something happening to Carrie. Dammit. He shouldn't have left her alone.

Coco barked wildly, so he bolted toward the sound.

"Sheriff's up to speed. Said he's caught up in something else, but a deputy will swing by as soon as he can. Said it might be a while," Kyle said from behind him.

"Does he know the guy he's been looking for might be right here?" Dade bit out as he reached her house.

"He didn't say."

The back door was locked, and Coco was going wild inside. Dade took off his shirt, wrapped it around his fist and punched out the glass so he could unlock it. If someone was in there he hadn't come through the back, so he wasn't worried about trampling on evidence.

Inside, Coco darted toward him, whining help-lessly. The dog running to him was bad, because she wouldn't leave a stranger in the house. Dade's heart pounded his ribs, and the thought of never seeing Carrie again smacked into him like a rogue punch.

Sure, he had feelings for her…intense feelings. But this was a whole new ballpark, and he realized he wanted forever. He'd messed everything up in high school and let her go without clueing her in. He wouldn't do the same thing twice. Dade would find her and tell her exactly what was going on in his mind, his heart. She could reject him and that would be okay. Well, not fine, but he'd learn to live with it. Not trying would cause regret enough to fill a life-time. And Dade couldn't live with that.

"I'll look out front. You good with checking the house?" Dade asked.

"Yes. Go."

Dade bolted to the front door as he heard the dis-tant sound of tires peeling out. And gunfire. Damn. He pulled his cell as he redirected toward his truck.

Kyle must've heard, too, because he flew out the front door. "There's no one here."

"You sure about that?" Dade asked.

"I'll double-check." Kyle immediately disap-peared into the house.

Dade called security.

A bad feeling settled over him when Timothy

Andover, the guard working this shift, didn't pick up. Dade climbed into his truck and started the engine. He flew down toward Timothy's post. *Come on. Come on.*

He tapped the steering wheel with his thumb as he gunned it.

Timothy's van was parked at the street entrance. His was the only vehicle. Dade roared up beside it and cursed when he saw the door open with the young guard splayed out on the floorboard, blood all over him.

Dade jumped out of the truck and immediately started administering CPR. Timothy was unconscious and he wasn't breathing. The hole in his chest was pumping blood. Dade cursed again in between rounds. The shooter must've used a silencer.

Dade fumbled for his cell and called 911. After relaying the information, he called Kyle.

His new friend made it in a couple of minutes.

"I gotta go," Dade said. "Ambulance is on its way. Out here that could mean twenty minutes. Will you stay with him?" Dade started to explain why, but Kyle was already shooing him away.

"Call me when you find her," Kyle instructed. "Let me know she's okay."

"Will do. Keep an eye on Coco for me. Make sure she doesn't get out." Dade's cell rang, and he fished it out of his back pocket after wiping blood on his jeans. He needed to go, but the other vehicle was long gone by now and he had no idea where to look.

"Sheriff Sawmill," he said, hoping for some good news.

"I've been apprised of the situation. An ambulance is on its way to your location," Sawmill said.

"Carrie was taken by the person who shot Timothy," Dade said.

"I've issued a BOLO, be on the lookout, for the person who took her," Sawmill said.

"Wait a minute, are you saying you know who it is?"

"Samuel Jenkins's aunt, Marla, has been found dead in a broken down RV on a remote corner of the Billings property on the outskirts of town."

"Murdered?" Dade asked.

"The cause of death is pending autopsy," Sawmill said.

"What condition did they find her body in?" Dade pressed. The name finally clicked. Samuel was the man from the alley on the first night Dade had seen Carrie again.

Sawmill didn't respond.

"Sheriff, you owe it to me to give me some answers. It might mean the difference between life and death for someone I care about very much." There were no ends to which Dade wouldn't go to find Carrie.

"There are no signs of trauma," Sawmill said.

"But she was wearing the warm-up suit that Ms. Palmer described as hers."

Damn. Damn. Damn.

"Ms. Hardin wasn't the only deceased person found in the RV," Sawmill continued. "A white male believed to be in his early forties was found as well. The cause of death is believed to be a gunshot wound, and according to the coroner, the victim has been dead for at least four days, maybe more. He fits the description of Nash Gilpin. Indications are that he was murdered elsewhere and brought here postmortem. I'm on-site, and there are pictures of Carrie taken in her shop and in her home pinned on the walls. The filling from a stuffed animal similar to the orca found on Carrie's property is pinned to the wall."

"Did Samuel kill Brett?" Anger roared through Dade for not figuring it out sooner, for not being able to protect Carrie. He remembered that Samuel had been in the shop the morning after the alley assault. He could watch her from his aunt's house across the cul-de-sac. He would have access to the house even with security roaming around.

"We found tranquilizers onsite and dosage information on giving it to a dog the size of Tyson and a person roughly Carrie's weight. There's chloroform, too," Sawmill supplied.

Dade issued a sharp breath. "Carrie wouldn't have

thought anything about him knocking on the door. She might've thought he was scared or needed something."

"A half-used roll of gauze with a fake blood vial from one of those party supply stores is here. He might've given her the impression he'd hurt herself," Sawmill said. "We couldn't pick up DNA from the stuffed orca but I'd bet money this filling will match."

"Any idea where he would take her?" Dade asked.

"That's the question," Sawmill said in an uncharacteristic break of character. Dade could hear frustration in the man's voice. He'd let another murderer slip through his fingers. Maverick Mike's killer was still on the loose. The high-profile case brought a whirlwind of unwanted attention to Cattle Barge.

Samuel wouldn't hurt Carrie. Not right away. But if she fought too hard—and she would—he could end up hurting her in the struggle.

Voices sounded in the background.

"I'm being summoned and I need to go," Sawmill said. "Dade." A beat passed. "I'm really sorry."

"I know, Sheriff. If I think of anything that can aid the investigation, I won't hesitate to call," he said.

"Call my cell directly," the sheriff offered before severing the connection.

Dade relayed the information to Kyle as the ambulance roared onto the street.

"I can take care of this," Kyle said. "And then I'll make sure her dog's okay."

Dade thanked Kyle and then walked over to his truck, searching his mind for anything that might give him a clue. Samuel definitely wouldn't take her back to his aunt's place. That's the first place anyone would look.

Before long the sheriff would send a deputy to process the place as a crime scene and maybe evidence would be found, but Carrie's life depended on Dade fitting the pieces together now.

The roses. The stuffed animal. The summer dress. What did those things have in common?

And then it occurred to Dade. Samuel would take her on a date.

He knew exactly where.

Chapter Seventeen

The old fairground was a twenty-minute drive from Carrie's house and far away from downtown Cattle Barge. The place on the outskirts of town had been shut down for the past ten years or so but had been bustling once a year for almost a month at a time when Dade was a kid. As soon as he confirmed his suspicion, he'd inform Sawmill. The sheriff's current location was on the opposite end of the county.

Dade had never driven so fast. Questions pierced the quiet. Could he get there in enough time? Was she hurt?

She wouldn't go with Samuel willingly, and he had to know authorities were closing in. Did he realize that he had nothing to lose? Because that would mean life or death for Carrie.

Samuel was bound to figure out a few things on his own—like that he'd be the most wanted man in the county if they put two and two together. Maybe he realized someone had come across his aunt's RV and figured he had to act. The thought didn't do good things to Dade's blood pressure.

He parked alongside the railroad and kept a low profile as he ran into the dilapidated grounds. He wasted no time jogging the perimeter and came upon a silver sedan in the second lot. He texted the license plate to the sheriff. There was blood on the passenger seat.

The sun would rise soon, bathing the area in light. Dade positioned himself to come in from the west. Where on the grounds would Samuel take her? Dade's first thought was the Ferris wheel, which was the highlight of any fair. But it was also high up and would expose them too much. It would require too much power to get working and it would take a large generator for that. Dade doubted Samuel would go to those lengths. Maybe something smaller in scale. Maybe he'd had a favorite ride as a kid. Thinking back, there was the tilt-o-wheel, and it seemed like most kids loved any spinning-type ride.

What was the name of the other ride that had been so popular with everyone? It had been even more popular than the wheel ride. Dade remembered. It was called the round-a-bout. It had a bench-like seat with a metal bar that came down to secure riders. Hormone-fueled teenage boys took dates on it so their bodies would be smashed together when the ride spun in a circle.

Where was it located in on the grounds? And then

he remembered that, too. Dead center. It was one of
the big draws, and its central location practically
ensured that no one would pop in and out—there
was too much temptation along the way to entice
people to spend more. To the opposite side was the
midway. Across from that was the trail to the less
popular rides and fun houses. Pretty much all roads
led to the tilt-o-wheel.

Dade moved quietly through the high weeds covering the once vibrant scene, remembering there'd
been a time when this place had thrived. Happy kids
had skipped along the streets now vacant save for the
overgrowth that came up to Dade's belt. Rust covered
rides, and even though the property had been cor-
doned off and marked as no trespassing, it was easy
to access. Dade had the financial means to do something about that once this was all over. He needed
this place to be something other than a beat-up old
ruin where the love of his life… Was he admitting
what his heart already knew? Carrie was the love
of his life?

A resounding yes echoed in his ears. The noise
had come from a place deep inside him, and although he was the only one who could hear it, that
didn't mean it wasn't loud. Carrie was the person
he'd thought of when he was overseas. She'd been
the one he wanted to talk to, to laugh with. And as
corny as it sounded, he'd wanted to see her belly full
with his baby after he put a ring on her finger. She

seemed intent on fighting the chemistry between them, but he had to give it another shot. Would she walk away so easily if she knew how deep his feelings ran for her? If she knew that he wasn't going anywhere?

He scanned the empty grounds, trying to convince himself that this was no different than any other assignment. Except it was. This was personal.

He'd been an idiot. The first time he'd had a chance to tell Carrie how he felt, he'd been a jerk instead capitalizing on the chance, and he'd blown it big-time. But now? He was just being a good old-fashioned idiot. He of all people should know that it was impossible to go back and change the past. But letting it control his present and his future? That was about as smart as a piece of driftwood.

The good news was that he was never too old to learn, and he couldn't even go there mentally about the possibility of bad news when it came to Carrie. He needed to have another chance with her. And if she'd take him, he needed to make it right.

Dade checked his position against the sun as his cell buzzed in his pocket. He pulled it out and checked the screen. Kyle had called the sheriff and wanted to help find Carrie. Dade relayed his location and then he did what he'd done on countless missions…located his target.

The sight of Carrie caused his heart to stutter. Seeing her there, propped up on the broken-down carousel in that summer dress, sent his thoughts spinning. Her motionless body slumped over the safety bar sent rage thrashing through his body.

He drew on every bit of willpower he had to stop himself from charging over and taking her off that ridiculous ride. He needed to locate Samuel. The man had to be around there somewhere. Getting Carrie out of there and to safety was the only thing important to Dade.

Samuel had a gun. Dade had no doubt the desperate guy would shoot if he felt cornered. Given that he had no idea what other weapons Samuel had, charging in like a bull was an even worse idea, despite every muscle in his body fighting to do just that.

After changing his vantage point a couple of times in order to gather as much intel as possible, Dade surmised that Samuel had to be inside the control booth of the spinning ride, and he had to be working on something. If this was part of the fantasy he'd built up in his mind, he might be trying to get the ride working. Dade needed time to ensure Kyle made it to the fairgrounds. Going in alone would be a last resort, because if anything happened to Dade without backup, Samuel could kill Carrie.

His own family would be there in a heartbeat, but the ranch was too far and Dade needed support now. He could only pray that Carrie was still breathing. He quashed the unproductive thought. Samuel would want her alive so he could carry out his date fantasy.

Dade's cell buzzed again, indicating that Kyle was on-site. Dade directed his newfound friend to his location, advising him to keep a low profile.

After giving Kyle a minute to get up to speed with the situation, Dade said, "We need a distraction, something to draw him out."

"Okay, let's see. I can…" Kyle paused to think, but Dade was already shaking his head.

"It has to be me. I won't put you at risk." Dade's hand came up as Kyle started to argue. Dade's mind was made up. The guy who went in first had the best chance of being killed on any mission, and this risk, this mission, was Dade's. All he cared about was Carrie getting out safely.

Besides, Kyle had a kid, and Dade wouldn't be responsible for a son losing his father. "The way you came down on your son. Do you think he'll forgive you?" Dade asked.

"He already has." Kyle studied Dade carefully. "The trick is forgiving myself."

Those words, that truth, hit Dade like a stray bullet. He would chew on that later.

"Did you hear from the sheriff?" Dade asked.

"He's still on-site at the crime scene. It'll take him a while to get out here, but he said he'll come in without lights or sirens," Kyle said. "He wants you to wait for further instructions."

"She could die. Every minute I wait could cost her life." Having backup—the more, the better—

was good. But Carrie could be killed, and then what would've been the point? Dade had to move. Now. "I'm going in from the other side. I'll get him as far away from her as I can."

"As soon as you do, I'll move fast," Kyle reassured.

Dade patted him on the shoulder. "I appreciate your help. I owe you."

"No, you don't. Feels good to be part of something again." Kyle waved him off.

Dade could appreciate the sentiment. He stayed low as he moved away from his newfound friend. The point adjacent to the ride near the midway would lead Samuel in the opposite direction, away from Kyle and Carrie.

He'd need a distraction, though. What?

Dade preferred to face his enemy head-on. In this case, a blitzkrieg attack would be more efficient. It would be a mistake to think Dade could get to Carrie without Samuel knowing. Wherever he was, he'd be watching his prize.

The sound of an old engine cranking up billowed through the morning air. Lights came on.

Dade crouched low, the weapon from his trunk extended in front of locked arms as he backed away from the noise. Until he got a good look at Samuel and a vantage point to take him out…damn. His training had kicked in, telling him to take out the enemy. But he was stateside now, and the sheriff's words echoed. Samuel could have a mental disability. Some of the wind knocked out of Dade's sail remembering those words. He wouldn't shoot a mentally handicapped person, any more than he could shoot a woman or child.

So he would find a way to subdue Samuel instead if at all possible.

Pat Benatar's "Love Is a Battlefield" blasted through the speakers, echoing eerily as the car Carrie was belted into made its first rotation around the carousel. Her slumped body sent Dade's pulse racing, so he took in a couple of bursts of air and then slowly exhaled. He needed complete control of his emotions, and normally he could separate them from a mission. But this was Carrie, and he'd never forgive himself if he could've saved her and didn't.

Dade figured Samuel was at the ride's controls, so he maneuvered around the weeds to get a look. He stood there grinning, clapping like a child. The ride started spinning faster. Dade couldn't make out what Samuel was saying over the song's chorus. Sawmill had said that the fixated person played out a fantasy. Having a date at a fair included playing games.

Dade moved to the midway, which was located directly behind him. Since Samuel seemed to have been planning this "date" for a long time he would most likely have figured out how to power a game or two so that he could get the full experience. The fact that Coco had barked and yet Carrie hadn't made a noise led Dade to the conclusion that Samuel had used something—that same drug he'd used on Tyson?—to make her pliant. He must've put the dress on her while she was out cold.

Dade scanned the area, looking for something to serve as a distraction. What could he use? What would be important to Samuel?

Samuel's idea of a perfect date seemed to include the High Striker, more commonly known as the swing-the-mallet game. Dade figured it might be rigged so that Samuel could show Carrie how strong he really was. He must've seen the few times Dade had shown up as being emasculated. Damn. If Dade could only go back and change the past. There were so many things he'd do differently.

Dade needed to let it go, forgive himself like Kyle had said and concentrate on being the man he wanted to be now. He surveyed the area, careful to trace Samuel's steps in the weeds. If anything was out of place or sent up a warning signal, Samuel would be tipped off that someone had figured him out. Since Carrie's life hung in the balance, Dade had no plans to let that happen.

If he could make Samuel believe the game had been turned on by accident somehow…

He fiddled around with it and…bingo. The lights were set on a timer. Samuel's elaborate plans would play to Dade's advantage. If the lights turned on too early, Samuel might believe he'd messed up the timer.

Okay. Good. Dade could work with that. Next, he scanned the area for a good hiding spot. There was a basketball hoop next to one of those dart-throwing games. Dade could hide in between them, and when Samuel bent over to reset the timer, he'd strike.

Adrenaline coursed through him. He needed a minute to get his nerves under control. He'd never once balked on a mission. But then, he'd never been on an assignment this personal before. Taking in a fortifying breath, he decided to use the tension to make sure he didn't mess up. Adrenaline brought a clear focus as long as it was controlled.

He reset the time to light up in two minutes and then took his position. He fired off a text to Kyle letting him know what was about to go down.

Kyle immediately responded with a text telling Dade he was ready.

Two minutes passed. The lights blared. Dade held his breath, waiting for a sign it was go time.

The music stopped. The ride stilled. And it was now or never.

He took his position, careful not to leave tracks through the underbrush.

He'd like to be closer to the game and, to be honest, he wanted a better position to make sure Kyle made it safely to Carrie.

Seconds dripped by until a minute had passed with nothing. And then two. By the third minute and with no sign of Samuel, Dade's patience wore thin. He was risking Kyle's and Carrie's lives, and the weight of it sat heavy on him.

Maybe he should move to get a better look. But then, doing so could expose him if Samuel was kneeling somewhere close, watching. Dade already knew the guy liked to hide and watch.

Dade checked his phone again, waiting for a text from Kyle that Samuel was on the move. No text came.

He took in a sharp breath, needing to come up with a different plan. And then his phone vibrated. The screen said Samuel was on his way. He was glancing around, suspicious, according to Kyle.

As soon as Samuel came into view, Dade would fire off the text that told Kyle to move in. He waited.

Nothing.

Samuel's caution sent warning bells flaring.

Dade knew he would win on strength alone, but he had no idea what tricks Samuel had up his sleeve. He just needed the guy to show up so that Kyle could get to Carrie.

And then he heard the sound of movement in the tall weeds. Could be an animal. His cell was already in his hand and the text ready to go. All he needed was to see Samuel and then hit Send using his thumb.

Samuel appeared. Dade thumbed the button on the flat screen of his phone as Samuel began inspecting the game.

Dade stayed low as a confirmation text arrived.

Kyle was on the move. There'd be no more contact until Carrie was off the ride and safely inside Kyle's truck, unless she wasn't breathing, in which case Kyle would text immediately.

Even from a distance of twenty feet, Dade could see Samuel's rifle.

Patience won missions. Normally, Dade had an abundance. This was different, and his hands trembled from the adrenaline spike. He clenched and released his fingers…waiting. Controlling his breathing.

Seeing Samuel didn't help. Another shot of adrenaline coursed through Dade as he watched Samuel follow the power cord, no doubt looking for the timer. He was aware of his surroundings, watching for anything unusual. A hunting rifle rested on his forearm, but that was better than a handgun. It would buy Dade an extra second or two, which could mean the difference between life and death.

Samuel turned his back. The moment to strike presented itself. Dade flew from in between the games, launching himself toward Samuel with a primal grunt. He made contact with the back of his knees, and Samuel's head flew backward.

The two landed with Samuel on top, but Dade quickly disarmed the man and tossed the rifle as far away as possible. It landed with a click and a thud. Using his powerful thighs, he put Samuel in a scissor-like lock. Dade spun, reversing their position and was shocked by the smile on Samuel's face.

"If I can't have her, no one will." Those dead eyes would haunt Dade forever—especially if Samuel killed Carrie.

Dade drew back his fist and knocked Samuel out with one punch. He immediately located his cell and called Kyle.

"Stop. Whatever you're doing. Stop. He rigged the ride to kill her," Dade got out through heavy breaths.

Kyle shouted the curse word that Dade was thinking.

"Don't go near her," Dade said.

"Too late. I'm already on the platform."

Chapter Eighteen

"Samuel Jenkins is tied up with an electrical cord where those lights are," Dade told Sheriff Sawmill when he arrived half an hour later. "He was unconscious when I left him. Either way, he's not going anywhere."

Sawmill instructed one of his deputies to check it out.

"What are we working with here?" Sawmill nodded toward the ride.

"Dade?" Carrie's voice was weak and her head bobbed as though she'd had too much to drink, but this was the first sign of life. Hope ballooned in Dade's chest.

"Can you be still for me?" Dade asked her. If she so much as moved, the whole place could explode for all they knew.

The bomb robot was scanning the area, and it was slow going.

Carrie didn't respond. Her head lowered to her arms that were positioned across the bar.

"There are a bunch of wires underneath the ride. I have no idea what kind of device. I emptied Samuel's pockets in case he woke and found the cell I already handed over." Sawmill had called a bomb squad to be flown in from the city. He'd called in a few favors for the speed, and Dade figured the sheriff needed a win on this one as badly as he did.

A man covered from head to toe with protective gear urged them to step back.

"I have no plans to get in your way, but I'm not leaving." Dade folded his arms, standing his ground on the perimeter.

The officer started to protest, but the sheriff stepped up on Dade's behalf.

Time was the enemy and the bomb guy needed to get to work as far as Dade was concerned, not worry about him in case there was shrapnel.

"Killing his aunt most likely triggered this," Sawmill said. "We won't know for certain until we complete our investigation."

"If Samuel is familiar with sedatives, that could explain how he got past Brett's dog," Dade said, and the sheriff was already nodding.

All Dade needed was for Carrie to come out of this alive. It was time to pick up the pieces and move forward in all areas of his life. He'd forgive his father, himself. He'd build the life he wanted moving forward, a life with Carrie.

"I can't stay here this close in case…" Sawmill's

voice trailed off. "My men are looking to me as an example and they'll insist on joining me if I don't move back."

"Understood."

Carrie's head bobbed again, and Dade's heart clenched.

"Don't move. We're going to get you off that ride in a minute. Keep still," he warned and was grateful she listened. Kyle was like a statue on the platform, a few feet away from Carrie.

The sheriff moved behind the barrier that had been set up as the bomb team agent worked a joystick controlling the robot.

Tension was thick.

After what felt like an eternity, the bomb guy declared the area clear.

In the background, Dade heard the bomb tech tell the sheriff that the setup was a hoax, most likely a deterrent. There was no bomb, just a tangle of wires meant to buy time if Samuel's fantasy had been interrupted.

Dade sprinted toward Carrie. Kyle was already working the bar holding her inside the bench seat. EMTs were a second behind as Dade reached her.

Her head bobbed up, and her gaze locked on to Dade.

"I love you, Dade," she said as she held out her arms. Tears streamed down her face as she seemed to gain more awareness of what was going on around her. Samuel must've drugged her to buy her cooperation.

"You're safe now," Dade said and he didn't care who was around when he said, "I love you, too."

DADE PACED THE hallway in the hospital, waiting for word that he could see Carrie. He'd stalked past a dozen reporters three hours ago, and the place was humming with activity. Extra security had been called in to protect patients.

A nurse wearing a name tag that said Bonnie stepped out of Carrie's room after what had felt like an eternity. "She's awake and asking to see you," she said.

"Thank you, Bonnie." He'd put on a clean shirt and had washed off the blood from earlier. Thoughts of Timothy's death weighed on him. Dade had already put a fund in motion for Timothy's wife to ensure she never had to worry about money again. It wouldn't bring Timothy back or replace him, but it was the least Dade could do. He'd also spoken to Kyle about coming to work at the ranch. The family welcomed honest people looking to earn a living.

Dade took a few steps inside Carrie's room. His heart stopped at seeing her there, hooked up to machines.

The minute her eyes opened, he moved to her side.

She patted the bed for him to sit but he shook his head.

Instead, he got down on one knee right then and there. He took her hand in his.

"Carrie, you were my first friend. I didn't do right by you in high school—"

She started to protest, but he said, "Hear me out."

She nodded as a tear rolled down her cheek. He hoped that was a good thing, because he couldn't read her this time.

"I should've been the friend you were to me. Loyal. Caring. Kind."

Her smile brought light inside the dark recesses of a chest that he thought would always be hollow, empty.

"I have to live with my mistake for the rest of my life. The only way I'll survive is if you're by my side. I've never felt this way about another human being. You're home to me, Carrie. *You're* my home." He paused long enough to look into her beautiful eyes. "Will you do me the tremendous honor of sharing your life with me as my partner, my wife?"

"I love you, Dade, and I'm in love with you. I've had a crush on you since second grade, but—"

His heart free-fell as he waited for her to finish.

She repositioned on the bed, sitting up to really look at him.

"You don't have to do this," she said. "I'll be okay. I'll pick up the pieces of my business."

"I'm not doing this to save you. This is the most selfish thing I'll ever do. I want you to be my wife,

Carrie. To be mine for as long as I have breath left in me. Nothing here is the same without you. You're the only thing that's real to me. The only person I need."

A knock at the door interrupted them.

"Come in," Carrie said with a glance toward Dade.

Bonnie walked in carrying a large bouquet of flowers.

"What is this?" Carrie asked with a note of caution in her voice.

"There's plenty more where this came from," Bonnie said with a shrug. "Read the card."

Carrie opened the small envelope and read aloud, "'Our thoughts are with you. Can't wait for your shop to reopen when you feel better. Signed, the Houston family.'"

"Looks like you have a lot of people in the community who care about you," Bonnie said as hospital volunteers moved in one after the other, filling the room with beautiful flowers.

Carrie wiped away a stray tear and then smiled. It was easy to see that she was blown over from the kind gestures.

"I guess news is out." Dade couldn't contain his smile. "My family sends their love. They want to visit as soon as you're up for company. You're a celebrity in this town. You might as well get used to the attention."

"You're the only reason Cattle Barge has ever felt like home to me, Dade. So, yes. If you're still asking, I will marry you. I'll be your partner in this life and your best friend."

Those were the only words that mattered to Dade. He kissed her.

A sense of peace he'd never known traveled through him as their lips pressed together. The past no longer mattered. He could forgive his mistakes. He'd found the love of his life, and part of him had known it all along.

With Carrie, he'd found a real home.

* * * * *

*Look for the next book in USA TODAY
bestselling author Barb Han's*
CRISIS: CATTLE BARGE *miniseries
later in 2018.*

And don't miss the previous books in the
CRISIS: CATTLE BARGE *series:*

*SUDDEN SETUP
ENDANGERED HEIRESS*

*Available now wherever
Harlequin Intrigue books are sold!*

COMING NEXT MONTH FROM

◆ HARLEQUIN®

INTRIGUE

Available June 19, 2018

#1791 BODY OF EVIDENCE
Colby Agency: Sexi-ER • by Debra Webb
When Dr. Marissa Frasier wakes up in bed next to her dead ex-husband, she turns to Lacon Traynor, one of the Colby Agency's best investigators, for help. In Lacon's protective arms, Marissa feels safe...but is the murderer closer than she imagines?

#1792 SAVED BY THE SHERIFF
Eagle Mountain Murder Mystery • by Cindi Myers
Three years after Sheriff Travis Walker sent Lacy Milligan to prison for murder, he's uncovered evidence that clears Lacy's name. Now the former enemies must work together to find the real killer—and time may be running out.

#1793 SWAT STANDOFF
Tennessee SWAT • by Lena Diaz
Partners Blake Sullivan and Donna Waters must put aside their differences and work together when the rest of their SWAT team is kidnapped. Sparks fly between them, but will they be able to find their teammates before it's lights out?

#1794 MAJOR CRIMES
Omega Sector: Under Siege • by Janie Crouch
Four years ago Cain Bennett ensured Hayley Green's arrest, and he's lived with the guilt of his former lover's incarceration ever since. Now, though, the people she was once trying to expose are after her—and only Cain can keep her safe.

#1795 RANGER GUARDIAN
Texas Brothers of Company B • by Angi Morgan
Texas Ranger Heath Murray and FBI agent Kendall Barlow must hunt down their daughter's kidnapper. But as they race against time, will they get a second chance at love?

#1796 RULES IN BLACKMAIL
by Nichole Severn
Someone is stalking prosecutor Jane Reise, and she knows she needs the help of irresistible former navy SEAL Sullivan Bishop. A tense shared history has him shutting her out, so she's forced to blackmail him. As her stalker closes in, they'll put their lives—and their hearts—on the line.

YOU CAN FIND MORE INFORMATION ON UPCOMING HARLEQUIN® TITLES, FREE EXCERPTS AND MORE AT WWW.HARLEQUIN.COM.

HICNM0618

"What are you saying? That instead of accepting that they could be lost in the woods, you think someone came up here and...what? What did he do with them?"

"No, I'm not saying that at all. I'm just throwing out the facts as we know them. The team drove up but didn't drive back down. They aren't answering their phones, radios or us yelling at the top of our lungs. Something bad must have happened."

Her voice was barely above a whisper the next time she spoke. "I think we may be in over our heads. We should call the station, get some volunteers out here to help us conduct a more thorough search. Even if they're not lost, they could be stranded somewhere, maybe in a cell phone and radio dead zone. Obviously something happened to them or their vehicles wouldn't still be here."

"Agreed. We need to get some help out here."

He raised his flashlight beam, training it straight ahead, slicing a path of light through the darkness of trees and bushes about twenty feet away. "While you make that call, I'm going to go deeper in to check that barn and the clearing in front of it. There have to be some footprints there, maybe a piece of torn fabric caught on a branch. I'd like to find some tangible proof that might show us where the team was last. The trackers will want to start from the last known position."

She shoved her cell phone back into her pocket. "We're not splitting up. I'm your partner. We'll check it out together. Then I'll call this in."

The wobble in her voice had him hesitating. He looked down at her, noted the intensity in her expression, the shine of unshed tears sparkling in her eyes. He'd been with Destiny PD since late fall of the previous year and had been her partner for over four months. In all that time, she'd always been decisive, in control, never breaking down no matter how tough things got. He'd never once seen her rattled. But right now she seemed...fragile, vulnerable. And he'd bet it wasn't just because she was worried about her friends. There was something else going on here. And he thought he knew what it was.

"Donna?"

"Yeah?"

"It's not your fault."

She frowned. "What's not my fault?"

"Whatever happened, whatever is going on with the team. I think you're second-guessing yourself, feeling guilty. But if anyone's to blame, it's me. If I'd been a good partner to you, we'd have both been here with them when—"

"When what? When aliens beamed them up to the mother ship? Come on, Blake. This is crazy. Four highly trained SWAT team members and the chief of police don't just disappear off the face of the earth. You know what I'm starting to think is going on? Group hysteria, or mass hysteria, or whatever psychologists call it. We're both feeding off each other's fears and making this into something it's not."

"I honestly hope you're right."

See what happens next when SWAT STANDOFF by award-winning author Lena Diaz goes on sale in June 2018 wherever Harlequin Intrigue books are sold!

www.Harlequin.com

Copyright © 2018 by Lena Diaz

THE WORLD IS BETTER WITH

Romance

Harlequin has everything from contemporary, passionate and heartwarming to suspenseful and inspirational stories.

Whatever your mood, we have a romance just for you!

Connect with us to find your next great read, special offers and more.